Killing the Horses

John Newsham

SALT'S MILL
BRADFORD

Killing the Horses
John Newsham

ISBN 978-1903110782

First published in this edition 2021 by Wrecking Ball Press

Design: humandesign.co.uk

Supported using public funding by
ARTS COUNCIL ENGLAND
LOTTERY FUNDED

CHAPTER ONE

Bradford, West Yorkshire.

'Shoot,' Liam said. 'You've got it.'

Ryan's finger tightened on the trigger but he paused. He watched the bird's beady black eye glance. He breathed and waited.

'What you doing?' Liam said. 'You've got it.'

The finger which warmed against the trigger was bony and pale. Ryan's hand froze in the autumn wind.

'Just wait,' he said. He narrowed his right eye. His left eye was already shut tight. He looked through the aim at the eye of the pigeon. It was as smooth as a lake and glossed with the morning light as the creature stared around, unknowing and alive.

A long moment passed as Ryan squinted at the bird.

'Shoot, then,' Liam said. He pushed Ryan's arm. He meant this as a joke but the shot screamed out and the pigeons scattered up into the sky. The flap of wings pealed in the white light which fell through the trees. Only one of the birds did not fly.

'What d'you do that for, you dickhead?' Ryan said. He jumped from the spot where he had perched and pushed his friend aside before running down the bank to find the pigeon. Liam followed.

It struggled in the mud. Its right wing flapped and its tripod talons scratched at the earth. It could not leave. Its left wing hung, useless by its side, where the rubber bullet had ruffled the grey. It thrashed and squawked while the two boys looked down at it. All the other birds had gone and the woods were quiet but for its shrill wailing.

'Oh shit,' Liam said. 'You've fucked its wing up.' His eyes were wide.

The screech of the creature was everywhere. Its cry accused them. Ryan looked around and the two boys avoided each other's glance. The bird continued to writhe at their feet. Ryan looked back and forth and scoured the woodland for something which he would not find. Leaves and mud in both directions. Trees further down the muddy bank. Trees further up the muddy bank. There was nobody else. The bird howled beneath him. He could break off a branch. He could try to find a rock. But what then? Could he?

He looked down at the pigeon.

He pointed the gun at it.

'What you doing?' Liam said.

Ryan looked straight down through the aim at the bird. This time he did not hesitate. With one squeeze of the trigger, the echo of the gunshot silenced the animal's shrieks.

For a moment the two boys were silent as they looked down at the dead thing. Three or four feathers had been thrown a short way into the air and took a few long seconds to fall.

'Oh shit,' Liam said as the feathers settled. He looked at Ryan, wide-eyed.

'Fuck d'you do that for?' Ryan said.

'I were only messing,' Liam said. His eyes were wide. 'I din't think-'

He did not complete the thought.

Ryan knelt by the dead bird and inspected it. It had fallen onto the side of its injured wing. The black spot on its back and another above its neck indicated where the rubber bullets had struck. He reached out and scooped it up using both hands. The air rifle that killed it hung from his right shoulder. He looked at the thing he had killed and felt its soft weight in his small hands. It felt like he had stolen something from above. Something which had fallen to the ground when it should have flown away. He looked around for something which did not exist and settled for something which did.

'Lob us that bag,' he said.

He nodded in the direction he spoke of. Liam turned to look. A white plastic bag lay, limp and damp against the mud, some yards back up the hillside. The wind had blown it there from somewhere. It was light with its emptiness and threatened to fly off upon the breeze once more. It carried nothing. Liam clambered back up the mud to retrieve it. He brought it to Ryan, parted the handles, and held it out like an offering.

Ryan lowered the lifeless thing into it and dusted off his hands against his jacket. He took the plastic bag from Liam. It was heavy with the body of the bird.

'What you gunna do with it?' Liam said.

'Dunno,' Ryan said. He looked through the trees and the pale morning light which clung like a layer of film to the estate below. He looked at the woodland on the hillside beyond. He looked at the field and the abandoned quarry where the skyline of trees had been scrubbed away. The layer of cloud covered everything but the layer of cloud was thin. Light shone high above it. School would have already begun. 'Could take it to the forest,' he said. 'By where they killed the horses?'

There was silence between them.

'Reckon your brother would mind?' Liam asked without looking at Ryan. Ryan did not respond. He parted the handles of the bag to look again at the dead bird.

They stumbled down the muddy hill in silence while some of the birds returned high above them in the trees. Wild light spluttered through the loose web of cloud. The wooded hills clung to the edge of the estate which clung to the edge of the city. Beneath the hills the rows of houses were quiet and still. A car drove by some streets beyond. A child kicked a football at the gap in a fence.

'How could he mind?' Ryan said as he walked before Liam.

'What?' Liam said. Ryan did not look back at him.

'Jamie,' Ryan said. 'How could he mind?'

'I just meant-' Liam's mouth searched for the words.

'Thick bastard,' Ryan said.

They walked through the forest in silence.

There was violence in the hillside. Each landscape carried its own violence, suppressed and contained in the veins of earth beneath it. Each landscape strained and clenched with a different violence. But this hillside carried violence more than most. It grimaced with its violence. It wore the face of one beaten and tormented. It wore the face of one ready for hurt.

The boys' steps crunched across the wet earth. Each step further taunted the stillness which misted through the lower trees. High above them there was movement. The upper branches swayed a little as the boys walked on. The pigeons perched upon the skeletal limbs of the trees like gargoyles on the ruins of some bombed cathedral.

Liam looked up at the birds as he walked. They stood poised in the trees like snipers. His mouth hung open a little as he looked at them. He glanced back and forth from checking his footsteps to checking the pigeons above. It was as though he had to keep them in his sights. His eyes were wide as his mouth remained open. The birds were above and he was below.

Ryan walked before him. He looked ahead a little. He looked down a little. He looked at nothing but the loose path formed before him through the mud and the leaves. The soft, persistent weight of the bird in the bag reminded him of its existence. He held it like some reason for being.

They walked on like this in silence. Ryan ahead. Liam behind. This was the silence which shivered into everything. The trees upon the hillside. The leaves that littered in the mud. The maze of streets beneath. The weary houses. This was the silence they came from. This was the silence to which they would return.

The silence seemed more at home in that place than anything else that moved there. It ghosted down the streets between the houses. Its roots clawed deep into the mud on which the two boys walked. It surrounded the estate with the hillside and the quarry and every other part of the landscape older than their thoughts could reach.

Liam broke the silence.

'Fuck me!' he said. His voice echoed off against the trees behind Ryan. A few of the birds fluttered, startled, through the branches.

Ryan turned around. Liam had stopped walking. He crouched close to the cold ground, looking down the muddy banking through the light to something Ryan could not see. His face was contorted with disgust.

'What the fuck's that?' he said.

Ryan looked down the hillside for whatever it was his friend could see. The streets below were glossed with rain but the rain had long since stopped. The houses looked wet. The houses always looked wet. They looked like they had roots which plunged deep into the earth and sucked up any rain that ever fell there. A car disturbed a puddle which pooled in a dip along the side of the road below. Ryan looked and looked. He could not see what his friend could see.

'What you on about?' he said.

'There. That.' Liam pointed.

Ryan looked again. This time he saw. He saw as Liam spoke the words. He saw the thing with his friend's disgust. It was some other kind of creature. Dead. Ryan saw the monstrosity of it. He saw it with his gut before his eyes, the way one sees something so cruel it should not be. The nausea of it hit him before he even knew that he had seen it. He dropped the bird bag with a soft plastic squelch against the muddy path. He staggered on straining legs down the steep damp banking.

Liam followed. His legs carried him down a little too fast with the gravity of the sharp slope.

The thing was a badger but it no longer looked much like a badger. It was nailed into the bark of a tree. It hung there, just above the height of the two boys. Black and white against the coarse, thick body of the tree. It was flayed out between two nails which pinned its two front paws into the rough bark. It faced the boys with underbelly bared. This made it look like a creature that had walked on two legs, like some mythic hybrid of beast and man. Its two nailed paws resembled outstretched arms. Its head lolled, useless and dead. Whoever had nailed the creature to the tree had pulled a noose of string around its neck. The string was tied off to nothing but looked tight enough to have killed the thing even without the nails. Its lower paws hung, dead, and there was an unmistakable deadness in its eyes. Its eyes remained open. Its fur looked soft and as real as if it were alive. The nails which held the dead creature into the living bark were rusty and thick and as real as evil. It was not clear if the string or the nails had been the first to drain the creature of its life.

'Who the fuck's done that?' Liam said. There was a flicker of some terrible sadness in his eyes which Ryan saw but did not want to see.

Ryan looked from Liam's eyes to the dead eyes of the badger. They stared down at nothing like a baby doll. They stared down, black and useless, at whatever it is a dead thing sees.

It was one thing to shoot a pigeon.

'Who do you think's done it?' he said.

Ryan knew who they were. The older boys. The same older boys who had killed the dog the winter before. He knew about that too. He was not the only one who knew but nobody told. They had said the dog was a stray but it was not a stray. Maybe it had once been a stray but it was the stray that used to wait behind Mrs. Kennedy's house. It was the stray that Mrs. Kennedy would leave scraps for and speak to when she was old and spoke to no one else. She had named it. Ryan knew this. He knew what she had named it. But he did not like to think about that dog. He tried hard not to think about that dog. Sometimes, though, he thought about that dog. The things he did not want to think about the most were the things he always thought about the most.

Now he would try not to think about the badger. Now he would think about the badger.

He looked at the creature with its arms splayed out. It wore its mortal wounds for anyone to see. He had shot a pigeon and he did not know why. He had shot a pigeon so the pigeon would not shriek and hurt. Something like that. Now he felt like he had killed the badger. He felt like he had nailed it to the tree to watch it die.

'They chopped a lad's finger off once,' Liam said. His words were matter-of-fact.

'What you on about?' Ryan said.

'Macca and Danny. Chopped a lad's finger off. The tip. Held his hand down and chopped it off.'

'Whose finger? You're thick as fuck.'

'Little Darren. That kid who used to live up next to my cousin. Him whose bike was nicked.'

'He was like eight. Why would they chop his finger off for?'

'Must've pissed them off,' Liam said. 'They're not right in the head.'

He nodded at the badger. It lent his point a certain weight.

'You're not right in the head.' Ryan said.

He noticed his hand twitch for the barrel of the gun. He wanted to turn and walk away but he did not turn or walk away. He kept on looking at the badger.

'It was them who did Mrs. Kennedy's dog,' Liam said. His voice was quieter though the forest was empty. 'Macca and Danny. You know about that?'

Ryan's eyes held on those of the badger. The sadness in the

animal's dead eyes reflected for a moment in his living ones.

'Come on,' he said and he pulled his gaze away.

He staggered back up the banking and retrieved the bag of bird. He glanced inside once more to confirm the dead thing was still in there. He told himself that it was his.

They walked a while further round the edge of the estate. The wooded hill enclosed the rows of houses as though they formed some ancient civilisation. But beyond that hill was Leeds. Beyond that hill were no invading forces.

They left the badger hanging from the tree and did not speak of it. Some things get hurt and do not ever recover. Some things die and do not come back.

The pigeons gazed down upon them. For a moment the sky was still.

CHAPTER TWO

This place was on the edge. The estate floated alone along the furthest reaches of the city's imagination. There was nowhere left to go beside the woods. And, in the woods, all bets were off. Everything was different in the woods. In the woods the earth made myths. Violent myths. Hungry myths. They moulded themselves from the mud. They had grown savage. They grew outside the edges, in the wilds and the half-wilds. Their roots meshed deep into the darkness under England's last neglected corners. Corners like this one. They had grown bitter and ugly and perverse, spurned by a land which had ignored them. But they grew, still, just as they had grown of old. Angry myths. Bloody myths. Myths that could kill.

Ryan and Liam walked on. Their boots collected mud. It clogged along the ridges of their soles. They walked like two pilgrims carrying the bird towards the field where they killed the horses.

'When'd they shut the quarry down?' Liam said.

'What?' Ryan said.

'The quarry,' Liam said. He nodded through the trees at the cavern of stone which cut through the far horizon. 'When d'you reckon they shut it?'

'How the fuck should I know?'

'But when d'you reckon?'

'I don't know, do I? It's always been shut.'

'Can't have always been.'

'Well, when d'you reckon?'

Liam thought for a moment while they walked on.

'Hundred years,' he said.

Ryan laughed.

'Are you thick?' he said. 'You think it's just been sat there doing fuck all for hundred years?'

'Din't you ever ask your dad when it closed?'

'Why the fuck would I ask him that for?' Ryan said. 'Don't ask him owt.'

'Why'd they shut it anyway?'

'Cos it's useless,' Ryan said. 'Look at it.'

They looked through the trees as they walked. Across the valley, the stretch of chiselled stone left a scar through the ground where the grasses gave out. Where the quarry had cut through the earth, the hillside opened out like the skull of one whose jaws were wrenched apart. A few new horses nibbled the wild grasses beneath it. There were not as many as had been killed the year before.

'A lad drowned up there once,' Liam said. 'You heard about that?'

'What you on about?' Ryan said. 'How the fuck do you drown in a quarry?'

'Used to be flooded allt time,' Liam said. 'But they drained it when that lad drowned.'

'You talk such shit, you know.'

'I don't, I swear. My uncle told me. He saw them drag body out.

He said he used to swim up there himself but then they drained it after that.'

'Well your uncle talks shite 'n' all.'

They stepped across a stretch of mud and did not speak. Their boots squelched into the sludge, violating the otherwise untouched stretch of earth. The path they followed was a path no longer. It was just a way. It was just the way with the fewest obstructions. They followed the way through the gaps between the trees. They followed the way through the places where the mud and the puddles were not.

The way led them along the crest of the hillside which walled off the northern edge of the estate. It led them down the hillside and back towards the level earth where the forest cleared out onto an open field. They slowed as the woodland thinned out. Beams of soft light pierced through the opening of trees before them. This gave the cloud-filtered sunlight the illusion of greater precision. They stepped out into it. It was vague and diffuse and everywhere once more. To their right was a road. It was desolate and grey and nothing moved upon it. To their left the field rippled up to the horizon. It was desolate and green and nothing moved upon it. There were no hills in this direction but the grasses sloped upwards so that whatever it was that lay beyond the field was out of view. This was end of the city. This was the edge of everything.

Across the stretch of field beyond them, the woods resumed. The earth swelled up into another hill which staggered upwards before them like a tidal wave. Up ahead, beyond the crest of the hill, was the quarry and the field where they killed the horses. The two boys could not see this from where they stood. They could see only the woods, towering before them like tomorrow.

The way across the open field left them mortal and exposed. There was a safety in the wood's anonymity. There was something protective about its stillness and its darkness. But, out on the field, the light which was white with the cloud was all around. The Yorkshire wind which came, untrammelled through the clearing, taunted the boys. They turned into it and towards the place where the forest resumed. They were fragile in the way the badger had been fragile. They were weak in the way the pigeon had been weak. The pigeon would not fly again. Other birds would fly but not that one. It was as dead as nothing and limp in a plastic bag. Things fall apart and easily enough. Life ends.

They staggered, wordless, into the living wind. The wind which slithered over the Yorkshire hills and down through the Yorkshire valleys was a sly shapeshifting wind. One minute it was subtle, like a memory of something you did not want to remember. The next it was everywhere, punching into your eyes, drawing the breath from your lungs, making you gasp, making you desperate, making you mortal and alone. It was older than the estate and the way through which the boys had stumbled and the nails which held the slaughtered badger and the gun which had killed the bird. It was older than the quarry. It was older than the word and it was older than the breath. Maybe it was older than time.

'Windy as fuck,' Liam said. The wind ripped the weight from his words and Ryan did not respond.

Out on the clearing between forest and forest, the wind had hardened the earth. The rains must have fallen here, too, but the ground had been battered solid by the open air. There was no mud and the boys' steps left no record of their wandering.

To the right, beside where the two boys walked, a knee-high fence cut them off from the empty road. On the far side of it, a dog sauntered down the pavement, moving contrary to the direction of the boys. It was a muscular little pit bull. It swaggered along like an escaped convict down the empty street. It turned its head to look at the boys as it moved past. Its eyes were violent and looked somehow shrewd and unintelligent all at once.

'Fuck me,' Liam said as he spotted it. His entire body flinched with the sight of the creature even though it was twenty yards away from him. He turned into the wind with a jolt and changed his step so that Ryan was between him and the fence and the road and the dog which ran alone along on the far side of it. The two boys kept walking. Liam looked past Ryan for the dog until it trotted down to the end of the street and turned left up another empty road. It waddled off, heavy on its legs, back in towards the bulk of the estate. Liam kept his eyes fixed, wide and alert, upon it.

Ryan looked at him and laughed. He laughed with exaggerated laughter.

'You scared of that?' he said. 'It's not gunna fucking eat you.'

'It'd bite me though,' Liam said. His eyes were wide and sincere. 'Them ones bite you allt time. My uncle got bit by one like that. Still got a scar.'

'It's a little short arse,' Ryan laughed. 'I'd knock it out if it tried owt. Fat little fuck. How can you be scared of 'em?'

'I aren't scared of all of 'em,' Liam said. 'I just don't like them ones.' He panted a little into the howling wind.

Ryan laughed again but the wind took the lightness from his laughter. All that it left was the menace.

They came to the next stretch of woodland. The riddle of its darkness unravelled through the trees before them like a myth in a language neither spoke. At the edge of the shade, where the grasses rippled out into a darker earth beneath the wood, a border of litter had gathered. The wind had blown it there to rest at the frontier to the fortress of trees. Carrier bags and an empty crisp packet. Three empty cans of lager and a label torn from whatever packaging had given it context. And, beyond them, the shadows. Ryan stepped over the rubbish and into the forest. Liam followed. A way emerged before them once more, climbing upwards again as the second hillside swelled out of the level earth.

'Wait a sec,' Liam said. The silence of the woods declared itself around them. Ryan looked back at him. Liam's eyes were wide and he looked as though he wanted to cry. He did not cry. His cheeks were red from the wind and his hands began to shake.

'What's up?' Ryan said.

'Just a sec,' Liam said. He lowered himself to a crouch a few yards behind Ryan. He brought his shaking hands up to his face and massaged his eyes with his palms.

'You still shitting yourself about that dog?' Ryan said. He tried to laugh but he stopped.

Liam held his head with his shaking hands for a moment. He looked past his knees at the black earth.

'I just don't like 'em,' he said.

'It's alright,' Ryan said. 'We saw it fuck off. Anyway, I've got this if it tries owt.' He gestured with the bag of dead bird for the rifle which hung over his shoulder. 'Thought you liked dogs anyway.'

'I do,' Liam said. 'Just not them ones.'

Ryan stood a few yards before Liam who continued to hold his head in his hands. A bird shrieked high above them in the trees while a car screeched past some streets away. The two sounds ricocheted against each other. Ryan looked up at the pale light above the high branches. Liam looked at the black earth. Ryan did not look at him and waited for the moment to pass. He traced the patterns of the branches high above him with his eyes. They looked like roots but they were up above. They were free. He looked back to the ground where the real roots swelled beneath the earth in which they were imprisoned.

'Come on then,' he said.

'Alright,' Liam said.

Liam pulled himself back to his feet and the two boys walked on. They followed the way further up the hill and deep into the woods. They did not speak for five minutes which felt like twenty-five minutes as they scaled the heights of their little Everest. They climbed from darkness into deeper darkness. Their boots slogged upwards through the mud until the forest breathed with their shortening breaths. They climbed through deeper darkness to the light.

At the crest of the second hill, the trees did not thin out but the light weighed in from all sides. The peak did not extend far before it tumbled away again and the forest stretched down to the field where they killed the horses.

The two boys stopped walking without speaking of their need to do so. They were out of breath. Their breath and the squawks of birds above them in the trees wept against the music of the forest. Light-headed and half-elated from the climb, the boys perceived the woods which sprawled around them as if the hillside had just been created. Woodland and mud and white sky and field below all glittered with the same strange light.

From the space where the boys now stood, they glimpsed the horses. The animals were nearer and larger now, meandering over the field through the branches off beneath the boys. The boys looked down at the horses like the birds must look down at the horses. They looked down at the horses like God must look down at the horses.

Almost wild, the horses roamed across the field in which they were contained. Their ears pricked from time to time, searching through the chaos of the cosmos of noise around them for some familiar command.

Only two were visible, down through the branches from where the boys stood. The branches framed the horses like a painting from centuries before. They looked as though they still wandered in some long-dead world where horses helped haul sandstone out of the earth. They looked more real than real through the lens of the intruding trees. Insistent and alive against the bronze grass, there was a magic to them. Magic was the word. Even if you had grown too old and seen what life could do, magic remained the word. It shimmered with the light against their coats.

The horse in the centre of their frame of vision wore a chestnut coat which gleamed beneath the soft light. It was fully grown but it looked so young. Its coat glittered like an incantation but its mane fell, matted and unkempt, across its head towards its eyes. Off-white strands of thick hair tumbled down past its ears like old rope.

The second horse was further in the distance off beneath them. This one looked younger still. It was brilliant and black. Mane and coat and eye and hoof were black, each competing to be blacker than the rest. Its black legs seemed to root the rest of the creature to the earth like the trees which loomed over the boys. Against the blackness, a dagger blade of white fur emerged from the animal's forelock and cut across its face down to its nose.

'How many are back int field?' Liam said.

'Fucked if I know,' Ryan said.

They stood and watched, spellbound by the roaming horses.

'How old you reckon they are?' Liam said.

'See this one here,' Ryan said. He raised a muddy hand to gesture to the nearer horse. The brown horse. 'That's not yet two yet.'

'How d'you know?'

'See its mouth, right,' Ryan said. 'Watch it while it's eating.' They watched the creature chomp at the dark grass. 'Watch its teeth, right.' They watched some more. 'Them aren't its proper teeth yet. It's still got its first teeth in. You know like what babies have?'

'Fuck off,' Liam laughed. He laughed but then he stopped. 'You can't tell that from up here.'

'Yeah, I swear,' Ryan said. 'Our Jamie showed us how. You age 'em from their teeth. He showed me with them old ones.'

'Them ones what got killed?'

Ryan looked past his friend's words to the young horse.

'Yeah,' he said.

He looked at the horse a long while and wondered for a moment what it knew and did not know. Then he looked down to the hand which pointed towards it. Then he dropped the hand which pointed towards it and looked down from the horses and down to the black earth.

Liam looked at him.

'What about that one over there?' he said.

Ryan looked at the earth some more.

'I dunno, do I?' he said. 'It's too far off to see.'

'What d'you reckon though?' Liam said. 'Look, it's eating grass now.'

Ryan did not look up.

'I said I don't know,' he said. He turned to look at his friend. 'You can only tell from its teeth. I can't see its fucking teeth from up here, can I?'

Liam stared through the branches at the horse and did not speak. Ryan turned and walked away behind him and off towards one of the trees. He stepped around it carefully, inspecting the litter of leaves and twigs and autumnal debris which lay beneath it. He circled the tree three times. He stepped around it with slow steps, looking for something which he would not find. He sifted through the loose leaves with the nozzle of the air rifle.

'What you after?' Liam said. He turned from the horses and stared up the incline of mud to where Ryan circled the tree.

Ryan did not respond. Liam's face was still red with the exertion of the climb. Ryan's face was pale. He sifted through the dead leaves with the gun that killed the bird. He stepped and he looked. He stepped again and looked again.

'Gunna bury it,' he said. He did not look at his friend.

'What?' Liam said.

'Come help me find summat,' Ryan said.

Liam stumbled over the cold earth in the direction of Ryan. Ryan continued to circle the tree.

The whole world ticked to the same strange motion. It was a physical law. Everything circled around something bigger. Everything aligned, now and then, around a moment. It happened more often than anyone could know. Moments like this one. Ships circled the globe, elsewhere. High above the boys, a plane carved its trail through the ocean of the sky. The boys did not look up to see it through the trees but the faint thrum of its four engines breathed against the edge of their awareness. It flew from somewhere to somewhere. Each somewhere ten thousand miles apart. Each somewhere a somewhere neither boy would ever know.

Ryan stepped slowly round the tree. The earth pursued its orbit through the blackness.

CHAPTER THREE

'What you burying?' Liam said. His words still wheezed with the exertion of his walk up the muddy bank.

'What d'you think?' Ryan said. He nudged the leaves aside with the nozzle of the rifle. He held the gun in both hands as if it were a metal detector which would guide him to some buried treasure.

'Pigeon?' Liam said. Ryan did not respond. 'What's point of that?'

The bird in the carrier bag lay still on the earth some yards below while the breeze trickled over it. It looked like a bag of meat.

'Just help me find summat,' Ryan said.

Liam stood at the next tree along from Ryan. Some twenty yards of living forest breathed between them. Liam's tree was shorter and thicker than the rest. Only a few of its leaves had died and fallen off. But it was autumn. Soon the tree would be bare and all would be dead.

Liam looked at Ryan for a moment with the same expression he had worn when he looked at the horses. Ryan continued to disperse the leaves around his tree. There was nothing beneath.

'Why you looking there for?' Liam said. He looked up. 'Just use this.'

Ryan looked down at him. Liam reached up to a branch which stretched out like an arm above his head. He strained upwards until he stood on tiptoes and held the outstretched limb with both hands. His face clenched in on itself as he tried and failed to snap the thick branch from the tree.

'Fuck are you doing?' Ryan laughed.

Liam did not respond. He rationed his breaths for the task in hand.

'Daft bastard,' Ryan laughed again. He continued to point the gun at the earth but his attention had been pulled from the leaves towards the spectacle before him.

Liam stopped to gather his breath while his hands still held the branch. For a few brief seconds he looked as though he might pass out. The forest around him glittered a little in his sight as he regained his breath. Then he clenched his eyes and his teeth once more and strained every muscle in his arms and back and willed each part of himself towards the precise and single goal of breaking the tree. The branch now arched down sharply in the boy's hands but still held stubbornly on to the thick trunk. It looked so unnatural it looked perverse, like the bent back fingers of one being tortured.

Something groaned from deep inside the tree. A pained, splintering cry emerged from the bark of the branch. Its thick skin was torn. It sounded like a fingernail being peeled slowly off.

Ryan stopped laughing. He stopped and stared.

Liam's face was redder than it had ever been. It was the face of a fat man of fifty and not a boy of fourteen. He strained once more and let out an anguished cry. His eyes slammed shut.

The splintering tore through the forest. The sound ripped along over the black earth and through the dry leaves. It bounced off the bark of a hundred other trees and ricocheted out from the hillside like a warning cry. It sounded like one, collective roar. It sounded like the anguished cry of all the lurking myths which lingered out of sight beneath the ground. All of the pigeons flew away. All except for the one in the bag which was dead and still upon the damp earth.

28

With a thud, Liam hit the ground. Bark and branch and twig and dying leaf came tumbling after him. His pain groaned through him as his body collided with the mud and the giant arm of the tree staggered down upon him.

For a long, thin moment there was silence. The tree towered over the boys, wounded and irreparable. Broken as it now was, it looked taller than before. It looked weaker and more vicious all at once. It stood like a judgement above them, casting a long shadow down along the mud which separated the two boys one from the other. Everything about the tree was out of balance. Everything about it looked strange and renewed and macabre. The silence which breathed through it sighed outwards into everything.

Then Ryan laughed. The laughter came through him. He dropped the rifle on to the bed of leaves and bent himself double as he laughed. The laughter startled the forest once more.

'You dickhead,' he said. 'Almost fucking knocked yourself-' his laughter prevented further words. 'You daft bastard.' There were tears in his eyes.

Beneath the branch which he had severed, Liam was flat on his back against the muddy earth. He groaned a little under his friend's laughter and struggled to lift his head through the thin twigs and leaves which splintered out from the body of the branch.

Then he managed to speak.

'Fuck's sake,' he said.

He pushed the heavy branch off his body with a groan and pulled himself up to his feet. Dead leaves clung to his jacket and hair and he dusted them off with his hands.

Ryan's laughter circled around a second time with renewed

buoyance before it drifted away into the silence of the wounded forest.

'You alright?' he said as he calmed himself.

'Aye,' Liam said. He was out of breath. 'Fell on me fucking arse,' he explained.

To demonstrate this point, he dusted away the mud which had accumulated on his behind with the palms of his hands.

'Fuck d'you do that for?' Ryan said. Joy still shone behind his eyes.

'You weren't gunna find owt to dig with ont ground,' Liam said. 'You can use one of them branches though. Easy as fuck to dig with them.' He straightened himself up with a little pride behind his words.

'How do you know?' Ryan said.

'My cousin showed me.'

'Your cousin?'

'Nathan. You know him. Big Fat Nathan.'

'Him who knew that lad what got his finger chopped off?'

'No, the one who lives round corner from you. You know him. The lad who got chased by them goats.'

'You talk such shit.'

'I don't, I swear.'

Ryan did not respond. He moved down the small ridge from

the tree where he had sought in vain for a branch. He walked to the level space which opened out before the tree which Liam had broken. He lowered himself to a crouch. He swept aside the dead leaves before him, clearing a surface of rich, black earth. He looked at the ground. Then he smiled and looked up.

'Why'd goats chase him for?' he said.

'Who?'

'Your cousin.'

'Which one?'

'Big Fat Nathan.'

'Oh yeah. One of 'em nicked his hat so he chucked glove at it. Then rest o' them ran after him cos he'd pissed them off.'

Ryan laughed.

'Worst thing was they nicked his glove after that cos he lobbed it at 'em. Only had one glove left by end of it,' Liam paused. 'And no hat.'

'You talk such shit,' Ryan laughed. Liam laughed, too.

Ryan swept the square patch of earth before him with the length of his right arm from the palm up to the elbow. The silent earth presented itself like an altar. Then he reached for the bag which carried the bird. The plastic was white and bore no writing. It was the kind of bag which takeaways and corner shops use. The kind where the plastic was too thick and smelt of plastic. It had grown damp and dirty where it had rested on the earth but it swaddled the bird and concealed the existence of its death.

Ryan unpeeled the plastic with careful hands. It crinkled with a crisp, white sound against the whisper of the wind through the forest. He parted the limp handles and looked down at the body of the bird. He looked at it a long while and did not speak. Living birds squawked among the branches high above.

He reached down and lifted the bird out of the bag. He cradled it in his arms for a moment. When he was certain that it was dead and that was all it was, he held it against his chest. Liam looked at him and then looked away. Ryan looked at the black earth.

'Ry,' Liam said. Ryan did not respond. 'Ry,' Liam said again.

'What?'

'Why d'you want to bury it for, anyway?' Liam said. His voice was careful and soft.

'Dunno,' Ryan said.

'Why up here?'

Ryan looked at the bird he held for an answer.

'That's what you do,' he said. 'When summat dies.'

The weight in his hands was soft and heavy all at once. It was soft enough that he could feel its fragility. Even dead, it still seemed fragile. It seemed as though it could die some more. But it was heavy too. It was heavy enough that he would miss its weight once he had put it in the ground.

'Why?' Liam said.

'Why what?'

'Why d'you bury it,' Liam said. He looked at the earth for his words. 'When summat dies?'

'Fuck should I know?' Ryan said.

'Reckon it's to keep it safe?'

'What?'

'So nowt gets hold of it?'

'What's gunna get hold of it?'

'Foxes or dogs 'n' that. Anything that'd eat it.'

Ryan looked at the bird again. He held it like a new-born child.

'It's not be gunna be safer int ground though, is it?' he said. 'Still gets ate in ground, just by worms instead of dogs.'

Liam offered an apologetic look to the dead thing in Ryan's hands. He looked as though he still believed the bird might fly.

'Why do you bury it then?' he said again. His voice carried some deeper fragility this time. Some stranger darkness. 'Why not just leave it somewhere, like when rest of 'em die?'

Ryan looked down at the bird in his hands. He furrowed his eyebrows a little before gathering himself and looking up at Liam.

'I told you,' he said. 'It's what you do when it dies.'

Liam offered another sad look at the bird. He looked as if he was about to ask some more but he did not.

'It's just summat to do,' Ryan said. His words held the hint of a plea. 'What else we gunna do with it? It's dead, int it?'

Liam shrugged his shoulders and did not say anything more.

Ryan cradled the bird down onto the cold mud beside the plastic bag. He stood up and tried not to look at it.

'Help us dig then,' he said.

Liam made his way towards the branch which he had broken. Through the rustle of the dying leaves, he snapped two branches from the severed arm of the giant tree. He walked back over to Ryan and handed him the thicker of the two branches.

'How the fuck you meant to dig with that?' Ryan said.

'It's well easy,' Liam said. 'Watch.' The pride returned to his voice.

He plucked a few remaining twigs and leaves from the branch he held before positioning it at a narrow angle against the black earth. He held it like a spear. He held it as if preparing for a sacrifice.

'Jam it like that,' he said. He broke the earth with the point of the branch. 'Then, when you push it into ground, just shove it down like that and allt mud comes out.' The spear of the branch cut easily into the earth as he spoke. He pushed the length of it which remained above the ground downwards so it slid through the damp soil. The thick, caking earth yielded upwards and spilled out of the ground into a heap.

'Nice one,' Ryan said.

Liam leveraged the earth out of itself again as Ryan watched. It looked like the ground was no longer quite solid as it churned and hollowed itself out beneath. Ryan reached for the second branch and tried to join in with the digging.

But he could not do it.

He struck the branch into the earth easily enough. But when he pushed it down against the ground as Liam had done, the mud would not give way. He looked down at the narrow dent of earth he had managed to loosen. It was scarcely a scratch against the vast hillside.

'Fuck's sake,' he said.

He tried again. This time he jammed the branch downwards like a blade into the body of an animal. There was no precision or awareness behind the strike. It struck hard against the solid mud and splintered a little with the impact. This time the earth tensed up. It gained greater solidity. None of the mud was dislodged.

'Fuck this,' Ryan said. He snapped the branch clean in two.

Liam continued to lever out great, soft chunks of the earth. He looked up at his friend while he did so. He did not speak. He looked at Ryan the way he had looked at the horses but with a deeper concern. He looked back to the ground which he shovelled without pattern beneath.

Ryan leant forward and put his palms flat against the earth with his fingers splayed outwards. Then he clawed into the ground as if sinking his nails into an animal's hide. He clawed down until his knuckles whitened and the tips of his fingers disappeared into the blackness. He did not stop clenching until he had a hold of two great, brick-sized lumps of earth. Then he wrenched them up and out of the hillside. He knelt, looking at the earth with savage eyes, and held the chunks of black flesh in his hands. He loosened his grip and let the mud dissolve into a loose dust which glittered down onto the ground. The earth seemed to bleed beneath him.

He launched down again, claws bare. His fingernails punctured the skin once more. He held firm. When he pulled his hands out this time, he held even bigger chunks of earth. In each hand was a great black slab, heavy against the muscles of his arms. He held them like great rocks of onyx or coal. Then he threw the chunks onto the ground and watched them shatter like everything shatters. He felt like an animal. He felt like a god.

He looked at his blackened hands and at the earth. He felt the glimmer of a sadness so terrible it would have destroyed him had it not dissipated the moment it arrived. He was out of breath and the earth was deep and dark. He panted a little and looked at the ground.

Between the two boys, they scraped away a shallow trench of earth some six or seven inches deep. It was longer than it was wide. It looked about the size of a shoebox. It looked like nothing at all. It did not look like the kind of place where something should go after it had breathed and been and flown over the earth. It did not look like anything that had ever lived should go down there.

It looked like a black hole in the ground.

Ryan reached forward once more and smoothed the ground of the shallow grave with the palms of his hands. He looked like he was levelling some ancient font out of clay.

'That'll do,' he said. He was out of breath.

Liam stood back to watch him. He leant at a slight crouch into the length of branch which he held like a shepherd's staff. Overhead, a crow cried out. The cry leapt out of the instinct of its black lungs and echoed through the forest. The sun bled through the clouds for just a moment before the cloud thickened again. The two boys looked at the empty grave.

'Aright,' Ryan said in answer to nothing.

He lifted the dead bird with his dirty hands and offered it into the muddy grave. Both boys paused to look at the limp creature for a long moment.

'Not gunna show your dad?' Liam said.

Ryan looked at the bird in the ground.

'Why would I want to show him for?'

'You know. Show him you got one.'

Ryan looked at the bird in the ground.

'He wun't see it,' he said. 'Don't see him til Sunday.'

'I don't mean keep hold of it!' Liam said. 'Take a picture.'

'What for?'

'To show him.'

'What's he want to see that for? Dead fucking bird?'

'Dunno,' Liam muttered. 'Show's you got one. I din't get one.'

Ryan looked at the bird in the ground.

'Take a picture to show your dad then,' he said.

'Don't be a dickhead,' Liam said.

The crisp wind offered no consolation and the trees were as neutral as stone. The horses continued to graze across the beaten field, compelled by the strange instincts of their animal minds. The city whirred along but the city was elsewhere.

'Sorry,' Ryan muttered.

Liam did not respond. He looked at the horses. Then he looked back into the ground at the bird.

'Lob some mud on it then,' he said.

'One sec,' Ryan said. Something in his mind had seen something in the deadness of the bird. He reached into the grave again with muddy hands and held the creature once more. He turned the thing onto its back and placed it carefully against the earth so that its limp head and empty eyes looked at the sky.

'Don't, Ry,' Liam said.

'What?'

'Don't put it like that.'

'What you on about?'

Liam looked at the eyes of the bird.

'Looks like the badger,' he said.

Ryan looked at him. He did not know whether to laugh. Then he looked at the bird. Then he saw the badger in his mind. Conjured clear as a vision before him, he saw the thing that had lived and did not have to die. He reached forward and placed his hands on the bird again. He rolled the creature gently onto its side. But for its damp grave and its dead eyes, it looked out from the hillside, down into the light towards the horses.

'Aye,' he said and he summoned a smile which took some effort to summon. 'Give the little lad a proper send off.'

He looked at the bird once more and something flickered in his face for just a second. Then he looked away from the bird.

'Come on then,' he said. He scooped up a thick mound of earth in both hands and let it trickle through his fingers and down onto the carcass.

'Nice one,' Liam said. He dropped his broken-tree staff and walked towards the piled earth beside the grave. He wedged a mass of soil down into the grave and over the bird with his trainer and his leg up past his ankle.

'Why you doing that for?' Ryan said. 'Use your hands.'

'Don't want to get mud all over my hands, do I?'

'Why not? Got mud on your back and your arse and your daft head as it is.'

'Yeah, but I'd have to wash my hands,' Liam said.

'Daft bastard,' Ryan said. He laughed as he held the earth in his hands and threw it down into the grave. He did not look at the bird. He looked at the grave around it. He looked at the soil as it piled upon it. But he did not look at the bird. He would not look at the bird again. Not as long as he lived upon the earth. He dusted off his hands against his jacket and then looked at them. Lines of black earth followed the creases in his palms. His hands read like two opposing pages of a map.

'See,' Liam said. 'Who's a mucky bastard now? My hands are clean.' He held up his palms and offered Ryan an expression of complete sincerity. Dead leaves still matted in his hair. His school trousers had bunched themselves up around his midriff, building to the point where his behind had first made impact with the earth. His crisp, white trainers were caked in thick mud. But his hands were clean.

Ryan smiled and shook his head at his friend. He said nothing.

He looked back at the ground. It bruised upwards like a black eye at the point where they had buried the bird. He looked at it a long while with his eyebrows furrowed.

'Need to smooth it out,' he said.

He leant down and made to reach for the ground with his hands once more. Then he stopped and straightened himself up. Instead, he stretched his right foot out and levelled the earth with his sole as if testing the temperature in a river. He stepped cautiously. The sole of the trainer on his right foot levelled the crude earth with as much care as if he was using the palm of his hand. Each time his foot made contact with the ground he pictured the bird, squashed and flattened in the dense mud some inches beneath. He felt the bird's body compress with the nerves in his own limbs. He stepped back. He looked with sad eyes at the levelled earth. The breeze carried the white bag away into the blackness and silence of the woodland behind them.

'Weird you can just walk on it, once it's int ground,' Liam said. His voice was matter-of-fact.

Ryan looked at him.

'What you on about?' he said.

'D'you never think that?' Liam said. 'Once you bury someone, they're just int ground and you walk all over ground allt time. You can just walk all over someone once they're dead and int ground.'

'You just worked that out?'

They stood beneath the soft, late-morning light and looked at the grave.

'Anyway, when d'you go walking over someone's grave?' Ryan said.

Liam ignored the question.

'What d'you reckon it's like?' he said. 'You know, dying?'

'Fuck are you asking me that for?' Ryan said.

'What d'you reckon though?'

'I don't know, do I? Fuck all probably.'

'What, there's just nowt?'

'I don't know, do I?'

'That what you reckon though?'

'I don't know, do I?' Ryan said. 'Why you asking me that for?'

'Just thought of it.'

'You're not right in the head.'

'D'you never think about that?' Liam said. 'Cos I do. Sometimes. Just wonder what it's like, that's all.'

The earth before them seemed to swell with the body of the bird once more though the ground remained flat. In the distance, the horses were alive.

'What you scared you're gunna die 'n' all?' Ryan laughed at him 'Scared some dog's gunna come eat you?'

'Course I'm scared of that,' Liam said. His eyes were wide. 'Aren't you?'

Ryan laughed some more.

'What, you're scared some little short-arse pit bull's gunna come bite your neck?' He said.

'Not that,' Liam said. His eyes were wider than eyes should be and he did not acknowledge Ryan's laughter. 'Scared of dying though. Aren't you?'

Ryan stopped laughing.

'I'm not gunna die am I?' he said. 'You're not gunna die. What you gunna die of?'

'No I mean like when you're old. You'll die then, won't you?'

'So what you shitting yourself now for?'

'Dunno,' he said. 'Just think about it sometimes.'

Ryan sighed pointedly and shook his head pointedly. Liam did not notice.

'Reckon you know when you're dying?' Liam said.

'Course you don't know,' Ryan said. 'How can you know?'

'You'd know like before though, wun't you? Like if you were sick, you'd know. If doctors told you you were gunna die, you'd know then?'

Ryan did not respond. He walked away from the grave and looked through the hills towards the horses.

'Hey, look,' he said. 'There's another one.'

Liam stumbled over to join him.

Ryan raised his right hand to gesture down towards the glimpse of new horse. He pointed with his entire hand as though the entire hand was needed to pay full respect to the great, lumbering creature.

The new horse was black and white. The two colours inked off of one another like the hide of a cow. There was something like wonder in Ryan's eyes as he looked down at the creature. There was a yin and yang to its blackness and whiteness which played off against each other in the motion of every kind of opposition all at once. Hope and despair. Order and chaos. Life and death. Everything played itself out across the body of the horse.

'Oh, nice one!' Liam said as he looked down at the creature. Both boys looked down as if watching some magic they could not quite believe in. 'What are them ones called?' Liam said. 'Black and white ones?'

'Piebald,' Ryan said. 'When it's got two colours like that.'

'Piebald?' Liam said. 'What's that mean?'

Ryan looked at him.

'Means it's got two colours,' he said. He mimicked the sarcasm his dad had used to joke with before his dad's life had all gone wrong. He wanted to speak the way his dad had once spoken. He did not want to speak the way his dad now spoke.

Liam looked at the horses.

'You want to go see 'em?' Ryan said.

Liam turned to look at him. His face wore the same wide-eyed look as when he had looked at the pit bull.

'Can't go down there yet,' he said. 'It's not safe, Ry.'

Ryan laughed at him but he was not convinced by his own laughter.

'What you shitting yourself for? We'll just go down to see horses. Be reet now, anyway. Them ones are all fine. Nowt wrong with it anymore.' He was almost convinced by his words.

'No, honestly, Ry, you're not meant to go in there,' Liam said. 'My uncle reckons they shun't have put them horses back int field. Said it's still not safe cos of soil.'

Ryan was able to keep up the illusion of confidence, the more fear he saw in the eyes of his friend.

'Since when's your uncle know about what's safe for horses?' he said.

'Used to keep 'em, din't he?' Liam said. 'When he lived behind field up by yours. I swear down, Ry. He said if them old ones were shot there shun't be any more up there for five years. Not 'til they know if soil's safe.'

Ryan paused for a moment. The fear threatened to bleed back into himself.

'What you worried for then?' he gathered himself. 'Not gunna be unsafe for us is it? Unless you turn into a horse.'

Liam turned away from Ryan and looked back down towards the horses. His eyes remained wide with his fear. But Ryan had outsmarted him. He was not a horse.

'Be alright,' Ryan said. 'We'll just go have a look at them. Just gunna see new ones, that's all.'

He walked back towards the taller tree to find his gun. Liam looked at the horses. Through the veil of parting branches, the creatures moved on heavy limbs over the thick grass. The field looked like it had not been touched by man. It looked like a land too wild to inhabit. The sky darkened just a little. It threatened to rain.

CHAPTER FOUR

The boys walked on, away from the grave and the mud and the black depths of earth and the soft light which shadowed around the tallest trees at the peak of the hillside. They moved down over the muddy bank that sloped through the woods toward the field. The horses moved beneath them. The field expanded out in every direction as they descended towards it. Everything about the horses grew in definition with each step. The alertness in their twitching ears. The gloss of their coats in the wild light. The sorrow in their lucid black eyes. Hooves, violent and dull against the browning grass. The steam of their nostrils, misting like a vision against the horizon.

The boys grew closer to the forbidden field like some terrible secret which stood, wordless and wild and alive and beneath them. A reverent silence overtook the hillside. The silence spoke of everything. It spoke of the magic in the horses. It spoke of the anger in the skies. It spoke of the sickness in the earth.

Then Liam spoke.

'My legs are fucking killing,' he said.

Ryan ignored him. He walked a few yards ahead of Liam. The hillside angled downwards such that a few yards ahead meant a few yards beneath. Ryan held the air rifle, still, but the bag of bird and the bird that had been in the bag were long gone. The boys looked like misguided soldiers stumbling down into some enemy sabotage.

'Hang on, Ry,' Liam said.

Ryan stopped. He turned to look up at Liam. Liam's face was pink and contorted into a pained expression a few yards up the hill behind him. The sun fell against Liam's face above the shadow cast by Ryan.

'What's up with you?' Ryan said.

'Let's just stop here for a bit,' Liam said. 'Just for a sec.' He panted with a little exaggeration as he lowered himself to the ground. He sat on a bare patch of mud on the open hillside. There were trees around them but the trees were fewer and no longer amounted to woodland. They could breathe the horses.

'Bloody hell,' Ryan said. 'You need to take up jogging, pal.'

Liam did not respond but panted a few more times as the pink in his face slowly softened. He looked down at the horses.

Ryan looked up at him then turned to look down at the horses.

'How about this,' he said. He raised his gun and aimed it down at the piebald horse. The horse moved around some thirty yards beneath them in the forbidden field. 'Ten points if I hit the white, twenty for the black.' He squinted through the aim at the horse.

'Don't, Ry,' Liam said.

'Reckon I could hit it from here though,' Ryan said. His words fell somewhere between a question and a declaration. He squinted through the aim and placed his finger on the trigger.

'Don't,' Liam said. 'Just leave 'em. Don't be a dick.'

Ryan laughed and lowered his gun.

'I'm only messing,' he said. 'Why'd I want to shoot horse for?'

Liam shrugged and looked down at the ground. His cheeks remained pink but the rest of his face had grown pale once more.

The minutiae of nature beneath him was as compelling as its

magnitude above. Tiny clumps of grasses emerged like miniature forests against the scrubbed black earth. The mud was drier here than it had been in the woods. The wind which battered the open hillside had punched all the moisture out of it. Some of the grasses survived. There was survival everywhere along the hillside. Survival was all that it was. Around where Liam sat, there were longer vines. They were not thick enough to veil him but the long, thin grasses clawed upwards around where he sat like bars in a prison cell. An insect he did not recognise crept slowly across one of the vines half a yard beneath him. He watched it for a moment then looked up at Ryan. He looked at the gun across Ryan's shoulder.

'What make's that?' he said and he nodded at the gun.

'It's not real, you div,' Ryan laughed. 'It's just a BB gun. Look at you shitting yourself.'

'I know it's not real,' Liam said. 'What make's it though?'

'Fuck should I know?' Ryan said. 'It's Jamie's. He had it for like ten year.'

The two boys were silent for a moment.

'My uncle shot a cow with one of them once,' Liam rested his eyes upon the gun.

'What?' Ryan said.

'He din't mean to,' Liam said. 'He said he was after me gran.' His face was sincere.

'What?' Ryan said again.

'That's what he says,' Liam said. 'He went to shoot me gran but missed and hit a cow. He din't kill it, like.'

Ryan laughed.

'Course he din't kill it,' he said. 'A fucking cow?'

'He said it were pissed off though,' Liam said. 'He ran off after he hit it in case all its mates ran after him.'

'Why's he shooting your gran for?'

'He din't shoot her,' Liam said. 'He shot cow instead.'

'Yeah,' Ryan laughed as he spoke. 'You said he were after your gran though. What's he want to shoot your gran for?'

Liam stopped and thought for a moment as if asking himself the question for the first time.

'Dunno,' he said.

'Int your gran like eighty?'

'Sixty-four,' Liam said. 'But this were like twenty year ago, when me uncle were a kid.'

He paused and his face was sombre for a moment as he looked across the field. Then he smiled and looked down at Ryan. 'I think he were just trying to hit her on her arse but she ran off. That's when he hit cow.'

Ryan now bent double laughing. Liam laughed too.

'He's fucking batshit,' Ryan said as he laughed.

'Yeah,' Liam conceded.

They laughed until the laughter ran out and the silence of the hillside returned. It was not really silence. Sound still bubbled around it. Above the boys, the wind blew ghostly through the highest branches. Their thinning leaves produced light whistles like the sound when a kettle boils. Somewhere on the ethers, the distant shore of motorway cars rippled endlessly by. But the silence remained like a physical thing. It was inarguable. It roamed across the hillside as slow and heavy and strong as the horses which grazed there. The noises which played off around it only lent it more weight.

Both boys were silent.

Liam looked down at his hands for a moment. Somewhere along the way the mud had dirtied them. They had not been blackened as thoroughly as Ryan's but they were tainted by the same earth.

He looked at them a long while and tried to gather the words he was about to say. He looked at Ryan. He looked back to his hands. He judged the moment with as much care as he could manage.

'They set one of them dogs on Mrs. Kennedy's,' he said. He looked at the palms of his hands and did not look at Ryan. 'That's why I don't like 'em.'

'What?' Ryan said.

'One of them little short-arse dogs. Set it on Mrs. Kennedy's dog,'

'Noah,'

'What?'

'That's what she used to call it. Noah.'

'Aye, Noah. They set one of them dogs on it. One of them ones we saw. That little fat fuck you said you'd knock out.'

'Pit bulls?'

'Yeah.'

'What you on about?'

'That's how they killed it,' Liam said. 'Macca and Danny.' He looked up from his hands and gave a cautious glance down to where Ryan stood beneath him on the hill. Ryan looked at him for a long moment as if trying to puzzle out some meaning from his words.

'No they din't, they shot it,' he said. He said the words as if trying to explain it to himself. He lowered himself down so he was sitting on the floor a few yards down the hillside from Liam. He picked up a long stick which had shed itself from one of the trees into the grasses. He plucked the remaining leaves and shoots which still clung to it.

'They din't, Ry,' Liam said. He looked at the palms of his hands again. 'They set one of them pit bulls on it. Tore it to shreds.'

Ryan furrowed his brow a little as he plucked at the stick in his hands. He turned the words he was about to speak over in his mind.

'You're full of shit,' he said. 'They just dragged it off into woods and shot it. They're fucked up but they're not that fucked up.'

'They are, Ry,' Liam said. 'Honestly, I swear to God, my cousin showed me video what they took of it.'

'No, they din't, they shot it,' Ryan spoke with urgency now. He pulled dead leaves from the branch with his bony hands. 'Like what we did with the pigeon.' He peeled back strips of the damp, dark bark revealing the pale core of smooth wood. It looked like a fractured limb.

'They kept cutting it, Ry. They tried to skin it but they din't know how. My cousin showed me video of it on his phone. It's fucked up. They tied it down when they did it so it couldn't do owt. Then they just went at it with knife. It were proper crying and trying to get away. I told my cousin I'd fucking grass 'em up. I don't even care. But he said don't be daft.' He paused. 'Then they set dog on it,' he said.

Ryan slammed his eyes shut and blinked back tears which were not there. He nodded to himself a little and swallowed hard before he spoke.

'Fuck grassing them up, I'd fuck them up,' he said. His head began to nod on its own as he held the barrel of the gun and looked at the earth. 'They're fucking little pieces of shit. I'd kill 'em. I don't even care.'

He nodded and rocked a little with his left hand tight around the barrel of the gun. He looked away from the ground and away from Liam and up towards the soft light which dimmed a little through the trees. The wind brought real tears to his eyes this time which he blinked away. Liam saw this for a moment and turned his eyes back to the palms of his hands.

'You can't do owt to them, Ry,' he said. 'They're psycho.'

'I don't give a fuck. I'll fuck them up,' his words were angry and the earth and trees glittered with an ancient sadness. He looked around for anything to steady the tremor in his voice. He settled on one tree in particular. Barren and skeletal at all but its highest reaches, it emerged, sombre and black against the pale light of the sky. It towered above the two boys a little way above them on the hillside. The height of it above them made them small and weak and young.

'Anyway that's why I don't like 'em,' Liam said. 'Them dogs, I mean.'

Ryan sighed an angry, empty sigh and did not speak. He was

about to say something but he did not. He sighed again. It was the kind of sigh that should arrive with tears but it did not arrive with tears. Then he gathered himself.

'Pit bulls?' he said. He continued to look at the barren tree.

'Yeah'

'Why the fuck don't you like them for? It's not dog's fault is it? It dun't know what it's doing.'

'I know but think what it can do,' Liam's eyes were wide once more. 'If it can kill a dog like that, it could fuck you up.'

Ryan now looked down at his own muddy hands. These were the hands which held the gun which shot the bird. These were the hands which held the bird.

'It wun't fuck you up if it din't get told to,' he said. 'It's a dog. It just does what it's told.'

His left thumb began to scour over the palm of his right hand. Clockwise first, then anti- clockwise. He tried to scrape the mud away but he could not.

'Not always,' Liam said.

'What?'

'Not always. Sometimes they just pounce. They do it for no reason. Once their head's fucked up they just turn and there's nowt you can do.'

Ryan slammed his eyes shut tight for a long moment and did not attempt to respond. His left hand now scratched at his right. Thumb against the palm. Fingernails against the whites of his knuckles.

The dirt of his left hand sullied the dirt of his right. He nodded to himself again and his upper body shook a little. Liam looked away from him and down at the dirt.

'If you know how to treat them right, they don't,' Ryan said. His words shook once more. 'If you look after them, they're alright.'

Liam looked at the dirt and did not speak for a long time.

'You been up here since?' he muttered.

'Why you asking me that for?' Ryan's sadness rippled out into anger but the anger was not enough.

'I meant since they put horses back up here,' Liam said. 'That's what I meant, Ry. That's why I asked you how many.'

'Fuck would I come back up here for, anyway?' Ryan said. 'You're thick as fuck.'

'I meant since horses were back here, Ry,' Liam said. 'That's all. I din't mean-' he stopped himself and looked at his knees. Then he looked at his muddied hands. Then he looked down to the horses. 'Why d'you want to go back now, then?' he said.

His words misted into the air like the breath from the horses' nostrils. The two boys did not look at each other. Ryan snapped the branch he had mutilated in two. The crack of the dead limb cut out across the hillside and startled one of the horses. The silence hurried back over it like a pall across the body of one just dead.

'I just want to see 'em,' Ryan said. He looked down at the two halves of the broken stick as he spoke, one in each hand.

'Alright,' said Liam. There was a generosity in the word which came from something deeper and older and wiser than he himself was. He was scared of the field. He was scared of the sickness which had got into the horses. He was scared that it would get him too. 'Let's go have a look then,' he said.

Ryan continued to stare at the branch he had broken beneath him. Its two halves were now indistinguishable from the grasses and the debris shed by the trees from the hillside. The paper leaves. The green shoots peeking through. The scraps of bark. The splintered branches. The living and the dead, mostly the dead, was all bundled and mixed up beneath.

He stood up suddenly and dusted himself off once more with his muddy hands. He forced a smile.

'Aye,' he said. 'Come on, then.'

Liam stood up and followed.

They did not need to descend much further until they were level with the forbidden field. A makeshift fence had been assembled by the farmer since they killed the old horses. Something unspoken forbade them from jumping the fence directly. It would have been easy enough to do so. In some places the wire mesh had been knocked down into the branches by the wind. In some places the fence ran out altogether and only a few thick branches and brambles separated the boys from the field. But they did not cross.

Instead they walked along the stretch of muddy path between the remnants of fence and the remnants of forest. They walked single file. Ryan ahead. Liam behind. They walked this way in silence.

They came to a clearing where the tracks of tractor tyres led across the way down to a wooden gate. The gate cut them off from the forbidden field. The gate was muddied and splintered and damp and a thick, rusty bolt kept the crossbeams firmly anchored to the post. Beside it, the sign was still in place. The one which the men from the council had left when they came to kill the horses. It had grown dirty with months of rain and wind.

A ribbon of red and white tape which had at one time stretched across the fence now hung and fluttered, angry and useless in the thick wind.

Entry prohibited! the sign read. *Control Measure Protection Zone ahead.*

'What's that mean?' Liam said.

'Means stay the fuck out or horses'll eat you,' Ryan said.

'Dickhead,' Liam muttered.

Ryan smiled.

The field waved softly down from where they stood and then up again with the slope of the colliding hills. It rippled off up to the quarry, clear and open in the middle distance before them. It spread out like an ocean concealing some vast leviathan. The violence of its surface could only hint at the darkness beneath. The clouds parted a little and cold beams of sunlight spilled out of the sky.

The wind came fierce and strong once more, down from the heavens and down into the open vale. Down through the hair of the boys, down amongst the grasses, down against the great, thick bodies of the horses. It howled like wolves at night. It thundered down like a stampede. It roared like an angry God come back to seek His vengeance. The boys and the trees and the field and the horses stood beneath like the damned and the righteous waiting to be judged.

Ryan stepped towards the gate.

Liam followed.

CHAPTER FIVE

Ryan climbed the gate's four wooden beams, shedding mud which had collected on his trainers before lowering himself down onto the mud of the forbidden field. Liam followed. He gave another cautious glance back in the direction they had come from. There was no one and nothing around save for the old tyre tracks which had hardened in the mud up to the gate. He lowered himself onto the field. One of the few new horses turned to glance at them for a moment before turning its weight back to nibbling its grass.

Liam gave another cautious glance back over the fence then stepped after Ryan. The mud on the forbidden side of the fence did not stretch far before it yielded to the grasses which sloped slowly up to the abandoned quarry on the far side of the field.

A laugh came through Liam as he took his first steps on the forbidden side of the fence. His fear lifted. His worries liked to accumulate and amplify to the point where he no longer felt them so much as he was possessed by them. He was scared of the man who owned the field. He was scared of the boys who had killed the badger. He was scared of the dog. He was scared of the sickness which had taken the horses. All the fears came as one monstrous body of dread which he could not comprehend. But it melted away as he stepped into the field, subdued by the gravity of the animals which lumbered across it.

It melted away, for a while.

'Fuck are you laughing at?' Ryan said.

'Dunno,' Liam laughed. 'It's alright this, int it?'

'Course it's alright, you daft bastard,' Ryan said. He laughed at his friend and shook his head.

The grass in the forbidden field was damper and the earth beneath the step was more forgiving. It seemed more forgiving. The boys stepped across it, trying not to disturb whatever monsters lay buried beneath. Their steps gained in courage.

The space between the boys widened as they tested the vast expanse of forbidden space. They moved apart like stars through blackness. Liam moved out ahead for the first time. The height of the grasses and the softness of the mud at this point forced the boys to take exaggerated steps until the ground levelled out to where the horses' mouths had trimmed the grasses down.

The wind subsided a little but the wind would return. They moved further up the gentle incline towards the brown horse and the piebald horse at the crest of the field where the field met the quarry.

Liam turned around with the unspoken awareness that Ryan had stopped. Ryan stood a few yards behind him, looking at his phone.

'Oh, fuck that,' he said to himself and put his phone back in his pocket.

'What's that?' Liam said.

'Nowt,' Ryan said.

Liam smiled at him. Ryan could see something formulating behind his friend's eyes.

'That your bird?' Liam said eventually. 'What's she whining about?' He smiled from ear to ear.

'Get fucked,' Ryan said. 'It's me mum.'

'Oh right,' Liam smiled. 'My bird then.' His face was triumphant.

'Get fucked!' Ryan said again.

'What's she want?' Liam said.

'Says I need to text me dad,' Ryan said. He looked past Liam to the piebald horse. 'Fuck that.' Ryan's finger twitched for just a moment for the rifle which hung across his left shoulder.

'Why don't you want to text your dad for?' Liam said.

'Why d'you think?' Ryan said.

Liam squinted and looked down at the grass for the words. Then he looked up, away from Ryan to another of the horses. This was the young brown horse which Ryan had told him was not yet two years old. The one with its baby teeth still in. Liam held his gaze upon it.

'Yeah, but he's your dad though,' he said.

'Fuck's it got to do with you?' Ryan said.

Liam shrugged his shoulders. He looked from the horse to the ground. Then he looked up towards the quarry. His eyes caught the rest of the horses.

'Oh, fuck me, there's loads of 'em.' he said. 'Look up there, Ry!'

This time it was his turn to gesture. Where Ryan had used the whole of his hand to point to the horse, Liam extended a single finger. He swept it along, tracing the line of horses against the horizon.

'Look at all them, Ry,' he said. The excitement was everything upon his face.

Ryan looked up.

'Oh, shit, yeah,' he said.

There were eight horses roaming against the horizon adjacent to the point where the crest of the field rolled up to the quarry. They scattered across the width of the field, each allowing the others generous space to tread and graze at the grasses.

'Let's go see 'em then,' Liam said, almost shouting to Ryan though the distance did not require it. Then he stopped himself. 'Reckon them ones are alright, Ry?' he said.

'Course they're alright, look at 'em.' Ryan said. 'I'm telling you, whole lot of 'em are alright now.'

'Alright,' Liam said.

They walked towards the horses. The breeze resumed a little. It was no longer as violent but it assured them of its strength. It hinted at a power it possessed but contained as it sighed against the grasses and into the faces of the boys.

The horses were every colour horses can be. There were two black horses and two chestnut horses and a white horse and a grey horse and a brown foal and a brown horse which mothered along beside it. Further down the field, by the small fence and the brambles which led to the quarry, were the first two horses they had seen. The piebald horse and the brown horse with its baby teeth. There were ten in total but up close it seemed like there were more. It seemed as though the horses were everything and all the rest of what was and what had been and what was yet to come was not quite real and did not matter.

'I like stuff what can't speak,' Liam said. He said this as if it explained itself. He tried to stroke the foal but its mother's eyes warned him away.

'What you on about?' Ryan said. He put his small hand against the body of the largest horse. The grey horse. It looked older than the rest. Something like wisdom joined something like sadness in its eyes.

'You know like horses and owls and foxes 'n' that,' Liam said. 'Stuff what just shuts up and gets on with it.'

'Animals?' Ryan said.

'Yeah, but, like, not just that,' Liam said. 'You know like ones what properly just shut up and get on with it. Like horses 'n' that. I can't explain it. You know what I mean?'

'Daft bastard,' Ryan said.

The old, grey horse accepted the cold hand against its back. It grunted a little and returned to eating from the earth. It was like an old tree. It was like an old mountain.

'You know what I mean though?' Liam said.

Ryan said nothing and Liam said nothing and the horses were wordless and brilliant and alive.

'Let's go see them ones then,' Liam said eventually. He nodded to the two horses which grazed further down the field by the brambles.

'Aye, alright,' Ryan said.

The field rolled at a gentle decline from the larger group of horses to the ones which had strayed. It was not steep but it sloped down enough to make it apparent that this was the way they should be walking. It lent an ease to their steps which followed the direction the hill dictated. Off in the distance, where the field gave out, the woods sloped down and the estate was beneath them. Beyond it was the road leading off to the school and the city and the world. It was all there, beneath.

'What are them ones called again?' Liam said in reference to nothing. 'Piebulls?'

Ryan furrowed his brow.

'Pit bulls?' he said.

'No them ones,' Liam said. He pointed. 'Them horses. Ones what look like cows.'

'Piebalds?'

'Aye, yeah,' Liam said. 'Piebalds. I like them ones best.'

'They're not called piebulls, you mad bastard.' Ryan said. He looked at him for a response which he did not get.

'Proper hungry,' Liam said.

Ryan looked at him as the two boys walked.

'You had your breakfast?' he said. When he heard teachers and dinner ladies and his mum speak to Liam, they spoke with concern. His voice aimed for the same but fell short. Liam did not respond.

They came to a stop by the horses. The two strays had strayed far from the rest. In their isolation they looked even more brilliant and alive. Everything about them was more pronounced. The bruising strength of their hooves. The gloss of light in the lakes of their eyes. Each thickened wisp of hair. Steam like the smoke from a furnace misting from their nostrils through the air.

'Why do they get like more than one colour?' Liam said. He put his hand on the back of the piebald horse. He was less cautious this time but he was still cautious.

Ryan shrugged.

'Dunno,' he said. 'It's like cows.'

'Yeah, why do cows get like more than one colour?' Liam said.

Ryan shrugged.

'Dunno,' he said.

'Funny that only some horses are like this, but all cows,' Liam said. 'Like, you wun't think it were strange if you saw a cow.'

Ryan looked at him. He thought of calling him a daft bastard again. He decided against.

Liam stroked the horse with less caution now. He stood close beside its head as he patted its neck. He saw the outline of his own head, globed and glossy and miniature, in the great crystal ball of its eye.

Some darkness emerged inside of him. He saw it first through his reflection in the horse's black eye. It possessed some part of him before the rest of him became aware of it.

'I don't reckon they should be back here, Ry,' he said. He looked at the horse. He stopped stroking the creature and looked at the palm of his hand as if it were stained with the animal's hide. 'We best go 'n' all.'

'What you on about now?' Ryan said. 'It's fine.'

Liam looked at his hand. Then he looked at the horse. Then he turned and stared, transfixed, at the cluster of horses which were further up the field. He looked at them as if looking at something that should not be.

'What if my uncle were right, though?' he said. 'What if they shun't be back up here?'

'Your uncle shot a cow's arse when he were trying to hit your gran,' Ryan said. 'What you listening to him for?'

'Knows his horses, though,' Liam said.

Ryan looked at him for a moment and stopped smiling. His eyes searched for something like concern.

'Wanna go have a look at the quarry, then?' he said.

'Yeah, alright,' Liam said. He continued to stare at the horses which stood like an unwanted memory against the bleak horizon. He pulled his eyes away and blinked a few times. He tried to un-see whatever it was that he had seen.

They walked away from the horses. They moved up the slow incline of field to the place where the field ran out and the wilds began. A border of nettles and brambles separated the horse-trimmed grasses from the path leading down to the abandoned quarry.

'Oh shit,' Liam said as he saw it.

'It's alright,' Ryan said. 'Just fucking walk through.'

His actions matched his words as he took his first confident steps through the knee-high brambles. He held his arms out to his sides and took large, careful strides.

'Argh, you bastard,' he said to a nettle.

Liam watched as Ryan made his way into the middle of the brambles. Then he weighed in after him. His steps carried even more caution and his face contorted itself into a perpetual grimace as he navigated the patches where the branches and brambles were not so high.

'Get fucked,' Ryan said to a bramble. The bramble did not comply.

Liam grunted and cursed with the scratches and stings that began to accumulate as he lumbered through.

They emerged from the miniature wilds and were silent. The horizon was soft and bleak and still. Where the wilds ran out, the earth sloped down a few short steps to the edge of the quarry. The ground beneath was acrid and dry. No grass crept through the hardened mud which had greyed with the years of stone being hauled out across it.

Up close the quarry was both bigger and less impressive than it had first appeared from the forest beyond. From the distance it looked long and thin, like a cut which would not heal. But, as it opened out before the two boys, it looked wider than a football field. It was not. It bit deep into the earth. Hollowed out beneath and before them, it looked like some gladiatorial arena or some gateway to hell. But there was nothing in it. There was nothing on the far slope of pebbled stone and there was nothing in the great, dusty pit below. The emptiness gave out beneath them like some portal to an underworld which had never existed. The boys looked down into it, searching for some deeper darkness. There was none.

'Told you,' Ryan said. 'It's a load of old shite.'

'What they used to do with it?' Liam said.

'Fucked if I know,' Ryan said. 'Dig stone out.'

'Dig stone out?'

'Aye.'

'Why the fuck they want to dig stone out for?'

'To sell it,' Ryan said. 'Why d'you think?'

'Sell stone?'

'Aye.'

'Who pays for stone?'

'Builders 'n' that.'

'Why'd they leave it then? Shit load of stone still down there.'

'Aye,' Ryan said. 'Worth fuck all now, though.'

'Why's it worth fuck all now?'

Ryan shrugged.

'Fucked if I know,' he said. 'Go try sell some if you don't believe me,'

Liam looked down into the pit. He tried to puzzle something out of all the nothing.

'Were quarriers all minted then?' he said. 'From selling stone 'n' that?'

'Dunno,' Ryan said.

'Must've been, though,' Liam decided. 'Digging allt stone out.

Must've been shit load of stone in that.'

'What you on about?' Ryan laughed. 'The ones who dug allt stone out weren't minted. They got fuck all.'

'Why?' Liam said.

Ryan furrowed his brow and did not know the answer.

'Its not gunna be them who dig it out who get allt money, is it?' he said. 'Be whoever owns it.'

'How d'you know?' Liam said.

Ryan shrugged.

'Don't sell it yourself, do you?' he said. 'You daft bastard. Just get your wages 'n' that.'

'What's point of that?' Liam said. He paused. 'I'd just dig allt stone out and sell it all, me. Get rich as fuck.'

On the furthest reaches of the quarry opposite, a scattering of pigeons came to settle on the grey-black rocks they camouflaged against. They perched for a moment and looked at the boys. Then they offered themselves back to the sky. They looked like rocks given wings.

'Used to use horses int quarry, you know?' Liam said.

'What? How do you know?' Ryan said.

'My uncle told me,' Liam said. 'That's what horses were for.'

'What you on about? When?'

'Like four hundred year ago. Summat like that. Whenever quarry were built.'

'You daft bastard,' Ryan said.

'I swear down,' Liam said. 'That's why they still got shire horses. Strongest ones, them.'

'They're not shires int field.'

'I know but you still see 'em all over, like.'

'What the fuck's horse gunna do down there? Kick stone out with its hooves?'

'They'd use 'em to lift it 'n' that,' Liam said.

'Daft bastard,' Ryan said.

They looked down into the empty space which opened out like a grave beneath them. If there was nothing beneath, there was nothing above.

'Why they still here now then?' Ryan said.

'Why are what still here?' Liam's eyes widened a little. He liked to be the one who asked the questions.

'Horses,' Ryan said. 'Quarry's been closed for fucking years.'

Liam thought about the question for a long moment. He looked down into the cavern beneath them at the shattered shales of useless rock.

'Dunno,' he said.

They looked down into the nothing once more. Then they turned and walked back towards the horses. The clouds were thinner and the sunlight sputtered through.

'Fuck's sake,' Ryan said as they left the empty quarry behind. They walked towards the brambles.

'What?'

'Could've just gone through there,' he said. 'Look at that.' He pointed. Further along, up the crest of the hill, the brambles had been flattened down where someone or something had passed through. A crude path had been formed through the miniature wilds of bent and broken branches.

They walked through the brambles and came out by the horses once more and felt as though they had crossed through some terrible frontier. The field and the green and the open space and the white sky were all around. The horses stood, huge and alive, against the bleak and brilliant sky. Life was intricate and infinite and devilish and wild. The horses were soft and strong and almost still. The day moved like water around them.

Ryan walked towards one of the horses. She wore a chestnut coat and her hooves were shiny and carried a hint of red like rusty iron. She raised her head to greet him. Her eyes were dark and knowing and sad. There was nothing across the whole earth sadder than the eye of a horse.

'Alright, girl,' Ryan said. He reached and stroked her forelock with his cold, small hand.

She whinnied her appreciation and he put his palm on the warmth of the space below her eyes. She looked at him for a long moment with her sad, dark eyes. Then she lowered her head once more, away from his touch and down towards the cold earth.

The horses stood close before the boys. There was no alarm or apprehension left in them. They lumbered around, trusting and quiet, and the two boys did not speak.

'Sure it's alright to stroke 'em?' Liam said.

'Course it is,' Ryan said.

Liam took a few cautious steps towards the old, grey horse.

'Aye, that one's sound,' Ryan said. 'Proper old, that one. He's calm as owt.'

Liam reached a nervous hand up towards the side of the vast body of the creature. He placed his palm against the soft, warm hide. He stroked the animal like the head of a new-born baby. His apprehension bled slowly out. The horse continued to eat from the earth and did not move or look up to acknowledge the boy. Its mouth let out guttural, complacent chomps at the messy earth.

'Nice one,' Liam said. He laughed with a little caution and a little relieved caution. 'This one's alright, you know, Ry.'

'Course it is,' Ryan said. 'They're all alright. Careful wi' foal though.'

Liam kept his eyes fixed firmly on the old, grey horse.

'Do little 'uns go mad?' he said.

'No, but it's mum'd get pissed off if you're not careful. Only cos she wants to look after it, like.'

'Oh yeah,' Liam said. He was more courageous now and took a small step closer to the old horse. He ran his hand up as far as he comfortably could towards the back of the horse's neck. He gave a few gentle pats against it. The pats he gave were heavy with the weight and warmth of the creature's giant body.

Then he stopped. He lowered his hands and looked carefully at the horse's head. Its mane was a darker grey than its soft-grey hide but it faded to a yellowish off-white. He looked down. Its hooves were weathered and yellowed and old.

'How old are they when they die?' he said. He looked at the horse and not at Ryan.

'Ones that aren't sick get to like thirty.'

'How old's this one?'

'Dunno, I'd have to see its teeth.'

'Have a look, then.'

'Nah, fuck off, it's eating.'

Liam watched the old horse eat from the earth.

'How old d'you reckon though?'

'I don't know. It's old though.'

'Is it thirty?'

'I don't know, do I? It's old!'

Liam turned away from the old, grey horse and looked past Ryan. He looked down the field towards the two horses which had broken off from the rest. The piebald horse stared straight back at him though it must have stood a hundred yards or more down the field. The glossy conkers of its eyes looked straight up the hillside to the eyes of Liam. It watched him the way that dreams watch the world of the waking. Wiser and stranger and deeper and more knowing and beyond. Further off in the distance, the brown horse ate from the earth.

'Why'd they have to kill 'em all for?' Liam said.

'What?'

'The horses,' Liam said. 'The ones what got killed.'

'You know why,' Ryan said. 'They were sick.'

'Not all of 'em,' Liam said. 'Some of 'em were fine. Your Jamie's were alright but they came and shot 'em all.'

'Aye,' said Ryan. 'I know.' He looked down at the grass. 'Once one of 'em's gone, though, the whole field's fucked. Nowt you can do.'

'Why?'

'Cos it spreads.' Ryan said. 'Gets into one of their heads and they can't think straight. Then it goes round whole lot of 'em.'

'But why din't they just shoot sick ones?' Liam said. 'Leave rest of 'em alone before they catch it.'

Ryan shrugged.

'Cos it spreads,' he said again. He was not convinced by his own words. He turned to look at Liam. 'It just gets right into their heads,' he said. He tapped his own head. 'That's what our Jamie told me. They look alright, but then it gets into their heads and they can't think straight and nowt's right after that. Can't even do owt. Just gets right into your head.' He tapped his head again. Then he lowered his eyes. Then he lowered his whole head to face the earth the way the horses lowered their whole heads. Everything was larger and heavier than it looked. The quarry. The horses. The field. You could pretend it was not all so heavy and crushing and vast but it still always was and it still always would be. Sometimes you remembered.

'You want to go see Piebald again?' Liam said.

'Aye, if you want, you mad bastard,' Ryan said.

They walked again from the larger cluster of horses down towards the two which had strayed. They followed the same way which they had already followed as if expecting the way to be different.

'Reckon we should go in for lunch?' Liam said as they walked.

'Nah, fuck that,' Ryan said. 'Too late anyway.'

'Could just go in for afternoon then,' Liam said.

'What's point o' that?' Ryan said.

'Lessons 'n' that,' Liam said.

Ryan looked at him.

'Why d'you want to go to lessons for?' he said.

Liam shrugged. He looked concerned.

'What else are we gunna do?' he said.

'Just stay up here,' Ryan said. His face was angry and lonely and sad. 'Shit all down there anyway.' He looked off down the field and down the hillside in the vague direction of the estate and the city and the school and the rest of the world.

Liam did not argue. They stopped when they were close to the piebald horse. It turned its head on its muscular neck towards them. The brown horse ignored them. It nibbled at the earth some way beyond.

'Got owt for lunch?' Liam said.

Ryan shook his head.

'Could just find an apple or summat?' Liam said.

'Fuck are you on about?' Ryan said. 'It's October.'

'So what?' Liam said. 'Not even cold.'

'Where you gunna find apple up here?'

Liam shrugged. 'Get 'em allt time,' he said.

'Yeah, int shops,' Ryan said. 'Not off trees.'

Liam nodded and looked down at the grass.

Beyond the horse was a small, crude fence which stood about the height of the two boys' waists. It had been built by the farmer to stop the horses from leaving the field. But the farmer had abandoned the idea before the fence was finished. It stretched only twenty yards or so back up the field, leaving the rest of the brambles wide open as a fence of their own.

Ryan walked past the horses and leant against the little fence. Liam followed.

'What happens if people catch it?' he said.

'What you on about?' Ryan said.

'If horses make people sick,' Liam said. 'Would it get in your head like that? Make you go batshit?'

'I told you, people don't get it. It's just horses what get sick.'

'But if it did,' Liam said. 'Like, if people start to get it, would it make you go mental?'

Ryan looked at the horses.

'Dunno,' he said.

'Would it mess you up?'

'I don't know, do I?'

'What'd happen if you got it though?' Liam said, carried away by his own words. 'Like, if you went mad, would you know you were mad? Would you get better or would you never see stuff right again? Would it always just fuck you up for the rest of your life?'

'Fuck are you on about?' Ryan snapped. 'I don't know, do I? You can't get it anyway, can you? Only horses. You're talking shit.'

Liam nodded and looked at the ground.

'Just shits me up, stuff like that,' he said.

The brown horse sauntered up to them and stopped near where the piebald horse was eating grass in the space before the boys. It moved with an irrational conviction, compelled by some instinct which dictated that one patch of open grass was better than another. It looked at the boys for a moment as it slowed to a stop a few yards before them. There was something like recognition in its eyes but its mind was as other as the mind of the moon. The two boys looked at the horse and the horse looked back at the two boys.

Then the horse lowered its head like an offering and nibbled at the rough grass.

Liam glanced up for a moment as a scattering of pigeons flew in no formation from somewhere to somewhere against the white sky. He lowered his eyes and looked at the point where the piebald horse's mouth met the earth.

'This where your Jamie hung himself?' he said.

The words came through him, unplanned. He looked at the piebald horse and did not look at Ryan. His eyes widened a little with the words he had just spoken. Ryan looked at the brown horse and did not look at Liam. The brown horse was the younger horse. Its eyes were more innocent and trusting and vibrant and unknowing and unspoiled. A long silence weighed down in from somewhere far beyond the field and the valley and the city and the horses. It stretched down and grew vast between the two boys for a long moment whilst the horses stood firm against the dark grass.

Above them, the pigeons were gone.

'Yeah,' said Ryan. 'Up in them trees.'

He did not need to point. The trees were black in the distance against the white sky. Their branches were bare. They shadowed over the roaming horses.

The brown horse stopped eating from the earth again. It raised its head as slow and heavy as a draw bridge. It gazed towards them, eyes black and sad and wordless and wild.

CHAPTER SIX

They waited a long time for something. They did not know what it was and even if they did they would not find it. Cloud thickened and bruised then thinned into a pale web before thickening again. Soon it would rain. The day would grow darker just like every day grew darker.

They waited and did not speak. The horses lumbered, heavy and mortal and alive, across the living grasses and the dead leaves. Ryan looked at his trainers, muddied and battered against the ground beneath. They met the earth a few yards from where the mouth of the piebald horse met the earth. The earth sustained them both, horse and boy. It sustained and nothing more.

Liam looked at the outline of the trees which were black against the skyline. From where the two boys leant against the ragged fence, the trees seemed to emerge out of the final line of the horizon where the field gave out against the white-grey sky. They shadowed in perfect outline against it. Black on white. They looked like cardboard cut-outs of trees like the ones in school plays. They looked like they lacked their third dimension.

Ryan did not look at the trees.

'What's biggest thing you ever shot?' Liam said. He looked at the black branches.

Ryan watched the grasses bending out from beneath his soles and he weighed up his answer.

'Dunno,' he said. 'Probably pigeon.'

'Yeah?' Liam turned to him with wide eyes. 'Should've took picture of it, Ry.'

Ryan shrugged his shoulders.

'It's only a pigeon,' he said. 'Can't shoot much else wi' this.' He raised the gun with little enthusiasm.

Liam looked at the side of his friend's face for a long moment and did not speak. Ryan did not look back at him. He looked at the ground.

'I've never shot owt,' Liam said.

Ryan looked up.

'You serious?' he said. 'It's piss easy with this. We'll go find a pigeon if you want?'

Liam looked up at the sad eye of the brown horse. The eye was black in its entirety but glistened with the globed, white sky.

'Nah,' he said. 'It's alright.'

They sat another moment in silence. The question came into Liam's head before he said it. He held it there a long while. Then he said it.

'What they shoot horses with?'

Ryan looked up from the grass and straight at the head of the piebald horse. Then he looked away and found himself looking straight at the head of the brown horse. He looked at the horizon and found himself looking at the tree. He forced himself back to watching the piebald horse.

'Big fucking gun,' he said. 'What d'you think?'

'Yeah, but what kind?' Liam said.

Ryan shrugged.

'Fucked if I know,' he said.

'My uncle used to have this big bolt gun,' Liam said. 'Kept it int fridge. I asked him what it were for and he said for his horse.'

Ryan turned to him.

'What?' he said.

'Kindest thing you can do,' Liam said. 'That's what my uncle said. Like if it's sick or breaks it leg or owt, just shoot it in head wi' that.'

'No, you daft bastard,' Ryan said. 'I meant, why'd he keep it in fridge for?'

Liam thought for a moment.

'It were fridge in his back yard,' he said. 'Not plugged in or owt. He kept all kind of shite in there.'

Ryan nodded. Then he frowned.

'Did he use it on horse?' he said.

Liam did not look at him.

'One time,' he said. 'On one of his shires.'

Ryan was silent for a moment.

'Why'd he need to shoot it for?'

'Cos it were sick.'

'Sick with what?'

Liam shrugged.

'He din't say,' he said. 'Just said it were sick and it were kindest thing to do.' He paused and looked at Ryan. 'You know, stop it suffering 'n' that?'

'How's that stop it?' Ryan said. 'Big fucking bolt through its head?'

Liam looked at Ryan. His mouth searched for the words.

'Well it's dead straight away, int it?' He said. 'Can't suffer any more once it's dead. It's just dead. Like wi' pigeon, Ry. Were alright once you shot it second time.'

Ryan sighed and looked at the ground. He nodded weakly. The musk of the horses mixed with the smell of shit and the cold anticipation of rain. The sky continued to grey. The boys did not speak for a long moment as the clouds gathered arms high above them.

'How'd he know?' Ryan said.

'What?' Liam said.

'Your uncle. How'd he know when it's worse to leave horse than to shoot it?'

Liam made to speak but then he stopped. He turned his head and stared past the two near horses for a long moment. Whatever answer may have existed hung way too far beyond.

'Dunno,' he said. 'But it's like with horses what got killed up here.'

'Them ones weren't suffering,' Ryan said. 'Like what you said. Most o' them were fine. Just shot 'em to stop it spreading.'

Ryan looked up at Liam. His eyes offered a plea for a moment. For a moment he was the one who was asking. For a moment he was the one who did not know. Liam looked back at him. He wanted to be the one to know. He wanted to be able to tell his friend the answer but the answer was somewhere far from the field and the boys and the horses if the answer existed at all.

The plea behind Ryan's eyes melted and gave way to something else. He looked at the ground.

'He wun't have shot it if it weren't right,' Liam said eventually. 'He proper looks after his horses.'

'I know,' Ryan said. 'I were just saying.'

'Anyway, it's alright,' Liam said. He spoke as if reassuring himself. 'My uncle says they don't even think about owt, horses. Like if you put gun up against their heads and just talk to 'em before you pull trigger 'n' that, they don't even know.'

'Course they don't know,' Ryan muttered. 'You thick bastard.'

The two boys were silent again.The brown horse had watched them this whole time while the piebald horse ate from the earth. It looked as though it had been listening to them. When it was contented that their conversation had stopped it offered its mouth to the earth once more.

Liam looked upwards. The clouds were thick and low above the valley.

'Gunna piss it down, Ry,' he said. 'Reckon we should go in?'

'I said I'm not off in today,' Ryan said. 'What's fucking point? Be shutting up by time we get down anyway.'

'Gunna piss it down though,' Liam said again. 'Could just go in for a bit.'

'You go in if you want then,' Ryan said. 'Do what the fuck you like. I said I'm not off in. I'm staying up here with horses. They're not shitting themselves about a bit of rain are they?'

'It's alright, Ry,' Liam said. 'I'll stay up here 'n' all. Just thought it might piss it down.'

Ryan looked at his shoes and the mud.

'Cheers', he said. He looked up at the horses and summoned a smile.

'Anyway,' Liam said, 'some of 'em are shitting themselves.'

'What?' Ryan said.

'You said they weren't shitting themselves,' Liam beamed with pride. 'Some of 'em are though.'

Ryan laughed.

'Daft bastard,' he said. 'Right, come on then, mad lad.' He stepped away from the fence and looked past the near horses off towards the bleak horizon.

Liam looked up at Ryan and then glanced in the same direction as him. The far cluster of horses seemed to have sensed the rain. They stood still with their mouths to the earth but they had congregated closer. They were ready for whatever storm was brewing.

'You wanna go see 'em again?' Liam said.

'Not them,' Ryan said. 'Come on.'

Liam followed Ryan with thick footsteps through the high grass until it levelled up to the cluster of horses who had chomped it down. He looked at the old, grey horse which stood like a shield before the rest of the cluster of horses. The old horse looked even more grey than before with the thickening cloud and the smouldering sky.

Ryan looked past the horses to the bare, black tree.

'Where you off?' Liam called to him. Ryan did not respond.

They approached the horses. Ryan walked ahead. Liam walked behind. The old, grey horse turned its head to watch them. It stepped forward a little and then stopped itself. It stood like a god before the rest of the horses. It stepped forward once more as if wondering whether to shield the boys or the cluster of horses. It stopped itself again. It shielded the horses. The boys walked past.

'Where you off, Ry?' Liam said again. Ryan ignored him again.

Ryan walked with a determination which came from somewhere beneath him, somewhere in the dark, poisoned earth. It was as though there was a magnet under the ground, guiding his steps towards the barren tree. Liam followed a few steps behind, breath quickening in his lungs.

'Slow down,' he said.

Ryan stopped. From the fence where they had leant, the horizon had looked as though it cut like a blade through the congregated horses. But they were past them all now. The horses were behind them and the tree and the horizon still lay further in the distance up beyond. The horizon was one of those illusions that lasted forever. You could walk and walk and walk towards it but you never came any closer. You just moved on to something else and something else and something else until your steps or your breath gave out.

The trees were closer now. The bare trees. The black trees which climbed above the far edge of the field. They were closer but they were still yet some way off. Their branches emerged like burnt embers against the grey ash of the sky.

'Were that one,' Ryan said. He did not point. Liam caught up beside him and slowly regathered his breath. He wheezed and raised his head to look at what Ryan was looking at. He was looking at the tree.

It was the furthest one into the field. It stood at a greater distance apart than any of the other trees. The other ones huddled together like horses. Their bony branches mingled and a few leaves still clung defiantly onto them. But not this one. This tree stood apart. It was stark and black and bare. Its bark looked so tough that Liam felt that he could feel it with his fingertips even as he only looked at it.

'Just if you were wondering,' Ryan said. He did not look at Liam. He looked up at the tree which rose above them some twenty yards beyond.

Liam did not speak. He did not look at Ryan. His eyes traced the tree once again, up from where the base of its trunk pulled at the earth, up along its coarse and frozen bark, up to where its branches splintered into smaller branches then splintered again and again, up to the furthest black twigs which bled into the sky like veins. The grey sky billowed beyond.

There was a strange comfort to it. The black tree. Even knowing what it had done. It was taller and stronger and older than the boys. Its roots clawed deep into the earth.

'Why'd he do it here?' Liam said.

A stiff wind came once more, untethered across the hillside. It punched into the faces of the boys and rippled through the branches of the barren tree. Then it died away.

'Fuck should I know?' Ryan said.

Liam said nothing.

They turned to look back at the horses. They turned to look back without either one speaking of their need to do so. The horses looked wilder from up here. Perhaps it was the black tree or the grey sky or the stern wind, but the horses no longer seemed like they could ever be directed or commanded. They looked more real than anything else that was. They looked as though they could burst out of life at any minute and into some wilder, madder, stranger new existence. Some existence where things did not hurt. But they did not. They remained as they were, as horses lumbering on heavy limbs across an autumn field.

'It's alright up here, Ry,' Liam said. He offered a cautious glance at his friend.

Ryan said nothing. He nodded as he squinted at the horses.

'Reckon these ones get apples on 'em?' Liam said.

'What?' Ryan said.

'Them trees,' Liam said. 'Reckon they grow apples? You know, like when it's apple season.'

'Apple season?' Ryan said. 'Why d'you keep going on about apples for? We'll go buy some food if you want.'

'No, I just mean do you reckon they do?' Liam said.

'Course they fucking don't,' Ryan said. 'They're not apple trees, them ones.'

They stood with their back to the trees which staggered into the sky above them.

'How d'you know?' Liam said.

'Cos they're not fucking apple trees are they?' Ryan turned to him. 'Fuck all on them.'

'Yeah but int that cos it's cold though?' Liam said.

'Yeah but there's always fuck all on them,' Ryan said. 'Just leaves 'n' that. Even in summer. Fuck all else.'

Liam turned back to look at the tree. Ryan still looked at the horses.

'Why d'you give a shit for anyway?' Ryan said.

Liam shrugged and looked up at the tree.

'What's point of trees what don't have apples?' he said.

Ryan turned but did not look at the tree. He looked at Liam.

'What d'you mean what's point?' he said.

'Like, what's it do if it's just got leaves?' Liam said.

'What d'you mean what's it do?' Ryan said. 'Dun't do fuck all. It's a tree.'

Liam nodded but the look in his eyes suggested he was still trying to puzzle something out of the tree.

'Reckon they know owt?' he said.

'What?' Ryan scowled at him.

'You know, like, cos they're alive 'n' that,' Liam said. He looked at the highest branches. 'Like horses. Reckon they know what's going on?'

'Daft bastard,' Ryan laughed. 'Are you fucking thick? It's a tree.'

Liam looked back at him.

'I'm just asking,' he said. 'Anyway, horses don't say owt or anything, but they know what's going on. How d'you know it's not like that wi' trees?'

'Honestly, you're not right in the head, pal,' Ryan laughed.

'Fuck's sake,' Liam said. He looked down at the floor and looked angry and sad. Ryan saw this. He stopped laughing.

'I'm only taking piss,' he said.

Liam nodded.

Ryan looked at the tree.

In the wind it moved as if with a will of its own. It looked deadly and knowing and alive. It looked at least as alive and as knowing as the horses. Perhaps it was as alive and as knowing as the boys. Perhaps it was more so.

Ryan stopped looking at the branches. Some ancient spirit which had lived among the grasses and leaves and branches of the hillside for ten thousand years or more now whispered along his arms. He tried not to acknowledge the thought but he acknowledged the thought. He looked back down to the base of the tree. Its roots pulled at the cold earth. It looked as though it sought to wrench the earth out from itself.

There was a knowing that went deeper than words and thought. There was the knowing that man had stumbled on and would not ever comprehend. There was the knowing that shadowed under everything. The mind. The breath. The word. The shadow stretched, dark and long and unforgiving, beneath.

Both boys looked at the tree.

'How's your mum?' Liam said.

Ryan shrugged. 'She's alright,' he said.

Liam looked at him.

'Yeah, but what about today though?' he said.

Ryan shrugged again. 'Dunno,' he said. 'She's alright though. Dun't talk about it now, like.'

'She come up here?'

'Fuck would she come up here for?'

Liam looked for the words.

'See tree 'n' that,' he said.

'She's not gunna be climbing fence to look at some old, fucking tree, is she?' Ryan said. 'Anyway, you're not meant to come back up here are you?'

Liam looked at him with wide eyes.

'I thought you said it were alright?'

'It is,' Ryan said. 'But sign says you're meant to stay out. If farmer finds you up here, he'll batter you. Dun't want to get fined.'

'Fuck's sake,' Liam said.

'It's alright, you mad bastard,' Ryan laughed. 'Just fuck off if you see him coming.'

Liam nodded and sighed. He looked at the ground.

'How's your dad?' he said.

'I don't know do I?' Ryan said. 'Not seen him for weeks. Why you obsessed with my dad for?'

'I'm not,' Liam said. 'I'm just asking.' He paused and searched for the words. Ryan's face and the sky gathered in readiness for the same storm.

'You ever show your dad owt you've shot?' Liam said.

'Why you obsessed with that for?' Ryan said. 'You can't shoot fuck all wi' this anyway. Only pigeons or sparrows 'n' that.'

'You've shot a sparrow?' Liam said.

Ryan shook his head. 'Too small,' he said. 'Tried once. They're fast as shit though 'n' all.'

Liam hesitated.

'Would you show your dad if you got a sparrow?' he said.

Ryan looked at him. His voice was no longer angry.

'Why would I want to show him for?' he said.

'Dunno,' Liam said. 'He's your dad, though.' He said this as if the words explained themselves.

Ryan said nothing.

A bird fluttered down from somewhere and landed in the tree above the boys on one of the tallest, thinnest branches. They looked up at it in a studied way. It was too small to see clearly from where they stood. It was a starling but neither boy knew this. The starling was alone.

'Reckon you could hit that from here?' Liam said.

'Yeah,' Ryan said. 'Piss easy.' He did not reach for his gun.

They watched the head of the starling flicker around as its bright beak let a bright cry out from its black lungs. Then they watched it throw itself upwards, weightless into the white sky. They watched it fizzle out into a tiny speck until they could see it no more.

'Right, come on,' Ryan said.

'Where you off?' Liam said.

'Come on,' Ryan said again. 'Got summat for you.'

He turned from the black tree and out into the winds. They moved into the open air and out beyond the horses.

The brown foal and the brown horse which mothered beside it raised their heads as one to look at the boys. Then they lowered their heads. First mother. Then foal. The mother's body and legs and head looked heavy beyond all heaviness but the foal leant, agile and light, towards the grass from which it ate. The wind grew and battered into the side of the mother horse but she held herself firm so that the foal felt none of this. It nibbled the dark grass, instinctive and contented and alive.

The boys stepped over the wide expanse of cold, unsheltered earth. The wind spat its curses down upon them. They moved across the field and back towards the brambles.

CHAPTER SEVEN

The boys and the reflection of the boys in the muddy puddle flinched against the wind which barrelled down across it. Beneath their feet the wind drew ripples straight across their dark reflection. Their shadowy likeness was rippled and distorted in the ground. The fiercest incantations of the winds moved past. The boys recovered the breath which it had stolen and the puddle retraced its imitation of the sky.

The puddle ran, long and thin, through the mud within the track cut by a tractor tyre. There was no way left here where a tractor could have driven. Perhaps it had been caught in the mud where the grasses gave way before the brambles at the edge of the field. The depth of the track which carried the puddle suggested the tractor had struggled to get out.

Liam looked down at the puddle's reflection. The muddy, watery form of himself looked up at him. Ryan did not look down. It looked like there were two more boys living in the cold earth beneath, shadowy and bodyless and wild. Liam looked up. He did not want to think about all that.

He looked at what Ryan looked at. The overgrowth of brambles was thicker here. It was nature at her most disordered. It was nature at her most vicious and untamed. They were further up the field now, far beyond the way which cut through to the quarry. The brambles here reached as high as the boys' heads. There was no way for any living soul to pass through.

'I aren't fucking going through there,' Liam said.

'Course you fucking aren't,' Ryan said. 'Wait here.'

He stepped towards the brambles. He was not looking for a way this time. He was looking for the place where the brambles were thickest. Their fingers stretched up and above him. He took a step in towards them, holding the lower branches at bay with his foot and his leg. He leant forwards and the brambles seemed to reach in around him like some monster enticing the boy into its trap. He swore and cursed and cursed and flinched as he tried not to anger the thorns. Then he steadied himself. He leant forward again, slower this time, with his back turned to Liam. Liam could not see what he was looking for.

'Fuck're you doing?' Liam said. Ryan did not respond.

Liam looked down at the puddle. The muddy specks of reflected pigeons cut through the reflected sky far beneath the reflected imitation of his head. They looked like some winged gods of the underworld. They looked like dead birds given flight once more, beneath.

Ryan cursed again and swore again and then returned, scratched and dishevelled and unfazed. With his arms extended beyond him, he grasped his offering with tight fingers. In both hands, bundled thick into his bony-fingered grasp, was a lump of blackberries which he had plucked from amongst the brambles. He did not offer them in cupped palms like a sacrament or prayer. He grasped them as though they were rats caught and writhing to escape.

The berries bled thick juice through the gaps between his muddy fingers and down onto the backs of his muddied hands. It looked like the blood of the earth and the blood of the earth was black. Ryan's eyes held a savage gleam as though he had just made a kill with his bare hands.

'Here you are, you fat bastard,' he smiled.

Liam offered a nervous look at the severed fruit. The bundle was as big as a heart ripped out from the brambles. It swelled and bled against Ryan's grip.

'Take it then,' Ryan said.

Liam cupped his two hands beneath Ryan's right hand and Ryan let the fruit tumble down. Liam gave a nervous look at it once more. Its blood was now on his own palms. Many of the berries had been squashed and had surrendered their shape in Ryan's grip. But others looked the way berries should look. Their waxy bulbs and ripening gloss activated some intrinsic part of Liam's hunger which had evolved some thousands of years before when his ancestors had roamed across the earth. He held it all before him like an offering.

'I don't reckon you're meant to eat these, Ry,' he said.

'What you on about?' Ryan said. With the muddy fingers of his right hand he plucked and ate the fruits still bundled in his left hand. 'They're fucking berries. Well nice 'n' all.'

Liam looked again at the fruit. He looked at it as if it contained some terrible secret he could not yet bear to discover.

'I mean stuff from up here,' he said. 'Stuff what grows int field.'

'What's wrong with stuff what grows up here?' Ryan said. He ate another lump of misshapen berries.

'What if it's still not safe?' Liam said. 'That's what made horses sick, Ry, eating stuff what grew up here. My uncle said it were soil where sickness comes from.'

'Well don't eat soil then, you daft bastard,' Ryan said. He squeezed one of the largest of the berries between his hungry thumb and fingers and shovelled it into his mouth.

'It's not that though,' Liam said. 'It's stuff what grows in it. Makes you sick when you eat it. Makes horses sick anyway.'

'What stuff?'

'Dunno.'

'Do what the fuck you want then,' Ryan said. 'Leave 'em if you like. I'll eat 'em. Thought you were fucking hungry though.'

Liam looked at the offering of fruit. It was black but it was not black like the mud or the grave where they buried the bird had been black. It was black like the hide of the black horse. It shimmered the same way. It looked perfect and alive the same way. It enticed the same way.

He scooped the mound of fruit from the bowl of his hands so that he held it in his left hand alone. Then he took one of the berries which had maintained its berry shape between the thumb and forefinger of his right hand. He held it in front of his face like a sacrament and looked at it for a long moment with quizzical eyes.

Then he ate the fruit.

It was thick and sour and sweet against his tongue. It tasted like the blood of the earth. The blood of the earth was almost ripe and only just a little bitter. The sweetness was everything but the sour, ripened tang lasted long after the fruit had been eaten. It made him feel more alive than he had felt before as though he had eaten something of the same earth that the horses ate from.

Then he ate again. This time he did not take a single fruit but a bundle of mismatched, misshapen fruits. He shovelled them into his mouth and chomped loudly and the black ink bled and stuck across his fingers and his hands. The taste was sweet and sour and sharp once more and his doubts bled out into the cold air.

'Get us some more, then,' he said. He ate the berries with full, contented mouthfuls the way the horses ate from the grass.

'Get them yourself,' Ryan said through a mouthful of berries. 'My hands are fucked from brambles.'

Liam looked past him at the mess of branches. Everything about them seemed to warn the boy to stay away. Their thorns were long and thick and they bundled like barbed wire at the edges of no-man's-land. He looked at his hands, black with the blood of the fruit. He made a vague attempt to wipe away the black ink by rubbing his palms together but this did nothing. The skin of both hands stuck together a little with the sugar spilt by the berries. He looked at the brambles again.

'Where's the berries?' he said.

Ryan turned and looked in at the forbidding mess of vines and thorns.

'Right down in middle of them branches,' he said. 'That's why you're not having any more.'

'Fuck off, I'll get us some,' Liam said. He looked with wide eyes at the thorny branches.

'Yeah, right,' Ryan laughed. He ate the last of his berries and wiped his palms against his jacket.

'Watch me,' Liam said. He spoke to convince Ryan but had not yet quite convinced himself.

'Go on then, you daft bastard,' Ryan said. He licked his muddy fingers and wiped his hand against his jacket once more.

Liam summoned a flash of misjudged confidence. He flung

himself towards the branches as quick as he could before his doubts set back in. He mimicked the method which Ryan had used. Foot extended to flatten the middling branches, left-arm shielding his face, right-arm elbowing the highest vines. But he did all of this in a burst of misguided gusto. The entire procedure was undertaken too fast.

As he stamped at one of the branches, another cut itself loose from a vine which had restrained it. It flung upwards like an uncoiled spring. It whipped at Liam before he could do anything to prevent it. The weight of the thick, thorny vine smacked across his torso and up against his right cheek. He let out a cry and lost his step against the lower branches. Ryan watched his friend tumble as if in slow motion onto his side and then onto his back in a heap of boy and branch amongst the brambles. Liam cried an animal cry as the branches reverted to their favoured angles in spite of the boy now nestled among them. Thorny limbs scratched at his face and nettles stung his hands and neck. He groaned like a fallen horse as his mind registered his new position down among the thorns.

'Fuck's sake,' he said.

The branches settled around him, satisfied that they had won. The stillness returned with the leaves and the nettles. Liam tried to raise his right arm but groaned and lowered it once more when it encountered a thorny branch.

Then Ryan laughed.

The laughter came through him once again but it was tempered this time by his surprise. He laughed and he looked into the web of branches for Liam's fallen form.

'Shut the fuck up,' Liam shouted. 'Fucking help me out.'

Ryan laughed again. The sound of Liam's voice, defeated and

disembodied among the brambles, was too much.

Ryan reached his blackened hand into the branches and pulled Liam straight out, up through the brambles and thorns. Liam groaned again as he passed through another veil of thorns and nettles and branches before he was out and up and standing on the mud beneath the cold light which offered no comforts.

'Fuck's sake,' Ryan laughed. He beamed at Liam but Liam scowled and did not look back at him. Liam gathered his breath and dusted himself off and looked at his hands which had borne the impact of his fall into the thorns.

Ryan paused and looked at the pained expression on his Liam's face. He struggled to suppress his smile as he considered his words.

'D'you get the berries then?' he beamed.

'Get fucked,' Liam said. 'You're always taking piss. Just fuck off.' He panted a little and blinked his eyes tight shut before opening them once more. He looked as though he would cry but he did not cry.

Ryan stopped smiling. Liam squinted, pained and red-faced, into the fading light beyond the trees. His breath grew calmer and they heard birds they could not see from the branches of some tree some way beyond.

'I'm only messing,' Ryan said.

'Well, don't,' Liam said. 'Stop being a div.'

Ryan, too, turned to face the light falling fast across the eastern sky. The sun still stuck somewhere high behind the cloud but its lowest rays sputtered out above the hillside and silhouetted the highest trees near the woodland where they killed the pigeon.

'Alright,' he said. 'Sorry.'

Liam did not say anything but his breath loosened a little and his face was a little less pained. He dusted his hands against his tracksuit trousers once more and looked at them. The nettles had left no trace but his skin still carried the sting.

'Fucking bastards,' he said. 'Why they got to have so many thorns for?'

Ryan shrugged.

'Stops fruit getting nicked,' he said.

'Fuck off,' Liam said. 'Stop taking piss.'

'No, I swear,' Ryan said. 'Stops animals 'n' that from getting it.' He paused. 'Din't stop us though, did it?'

He smiled. Liam hesitated. Then he smiled too.

A colder wind blew over the hillside. It carried the chill of the approaching winter. The darkness bore the same threat. The evening darkness at this time of year was a deeper darkness. It carried with it the reminder of the winter darkness which would soon devour everything. The berries would be taken by the mould. All the trees would soon be bare. Birds would fly south. Frost would suffocate the grasses. The weakest animals would die.

In the western sky, beyond the brambles and the empty quarry and the nothing beneath it, the horizon was draining the light.

'Reckon we should head off?' Liam said.

Ryan looked at the floor. His face was sad and lonely and angry all at once.

'Yeah, alright,' he said. 'Not yet though.'

'It's cold, Ry,' Liam said.

Ryan looked around the field with a little desperation which his face could not quite veil. He looked to the black tree. He looked back to the hillside where they killed the bird. He saw the cold light thinning through the branches. He looked at the horses.

'Let's go back downt path through woods then,' he said.

'Alright,' Liam said.

They stepped back over the hardening earth towards the huddled horses. The piebald horse and the brown horse which had strayed had returned to join the rest.

Liam limped a little from his fall. Ryan clenched the palms of his hands together, trying to rid them of their sting. The gun still hung from his shoulder. They walked back down to the horses like soldiers back from no-man's-land. The darkness crept slowly behind them.

CHAPTER EIGHT

'Here, right,' Ryan said as the two boys walked, 'would you rather fall into a shitload of nettles or get shot by BB gun?'

Liam did not stop to consider the question.

'BB gun,' he said. 'Them thorns hurt like fuck.'

Ryan swung the gun from his shoulder and into his hands and pointed the muzzle at Liam as the two boys walked.

'Come on then,' he said. 'Let's see which hurts more.'

'Nah, fuck off,' Liam flinched.

'I'm only messing,' Ryan said. He hung the belt of the gun back over his shoulder. 'This'd hurt more though. These hurt like fuck.'

The two boys kept walking.

'How d'you know?' Liam said.

'Shot myself ont leg once,' Ryan said.

'Why?' Liam said.

'See what it felt like,' Ryan said.

'What's it feel like?'

'Hurts like fuck.'

Liam nodded. Ryan looked at him. Something seemed to shadow over Liam. Something darker than the darkness which emerged from the mouth of the horizon behind them.

'What about this then,' Ryan said. 'Fall into nettles,' he thought for a moment, 'or get bit by that short-arse pit bull?'

Liam scrunched his eyebrows as he thought. The two boys kept walking. The warmth of the horses steamed into the cold air before them.

'Nettles, then,' Liam said. His eyes were wide with the memory of his fear.

Ryan laughed.

'Yeah, me too,' he said. Then his smile retreated. 'If you had BB gun and that pit bull were running at you, would you shoot it?' he said.

Liam looked up at him. 'If it were gunna bite me,' he said. 'Course I would.'

'What if it died?' Ryan said.

'It wun't die, would it?' Liam said. 'It'd just fuck off.'

'If you knew it would die though,' Ryan said. 'Like if that were your choice: you kill it or it bites you.'

'Dunno,' Liam said. 'Kill it then, I suppose.' He looked at the ground with sad eyes as they walked.

They came to a stop by the horses. The ten creatures roamed closer to each other now. There was still clear space between most of them but they all occupied the same segment of the field. Some huddled nearer to one another and shared in each other's warmth. In the cold air and the fading evening light, the steam of their nostrils gained clarity. A mist of wordless breath hazed from them.

The two boys did not speak for a long while. They breathed with the horses.

The old, grey horse looked older now than it had looked when the light was all around. Or perhaps it just looked weaker. Its body looked smaller than it had looked before. It looked as though there were storms which that body would not withstand. It looked like there were winters which would floor it. The way it raised its head to acknowledge the boys seemed more laboured. Its neck looked more fragile and mortal.

Beyond it, on spindly legs, the brown foal huddled close to its mother. The mother sheltered the little horse like a dry stone wall but the horse still shivered and cowered with the cold and the growing dark. The mother turned her head, wordless and sad, to face the eastern horizon where the light had all gone. Then she looked down at her foal. She lowered her nose to meet its head.

Ryan reached out to stroke the old, grey horse. Then he stopped and lowered his hand. He looked beyond to the mother and he looked at the foal, cowed beneath the coming dark. He turned to look at Liam and his face mirrored the retreating light. Some darkness bled out somewhere inside of him.

'Right, how about this,' he said. He looked back at the foal. 'Say you get bitten by pit bull, right. Say it's gunna properly fuck you up, just gets let loose on you and there's nowt you can do. Say you get that, right, or if you want to stop it,' he paused. 'If you don't want to get fucked up by pit bull, you have to shoot little foal. Right between its eyes.'

'Fuck off,' Liam said. 'I aren't fucking shooting foal. Why would I want to shoot foal for?'

Ryan shrugged.

'Pit bull's gunna fuck you up then,' he said. He looked at the ground and he paused. He did not look up at Liam. 'Wun't kill you either. Bite you all over, though. Bite your neck. Bite your eyes. Might bite your eyes out. But you still wun't shoot foal?'

'Don't be a dickhead,' Liam said.

'You'd shoot it if it were sick though?' Ryan said. 'You know, with bolt gun, like what your uncle's got?'

Liam stared into the purpling air as if the answer was hidden amongst it.

'If it were suffering 'n' that?' Liam said. 'Then I would.'

His eyes were less decisive than his words.

'How d'you know when it's suffering enough?' Ryan said.

'Ask vet,' Liam said.

'How's vet know?' Ryan said. 'Vet can't get in horse's head can it?'

'I don't know, do I?' Liam said. His words were angry but the anger was unconvincing. 'You asked question.'

'Alright, don't shit yourself,' Ryan said. 'It's just a game.'

They looked at the mother and the foal and did not speak for a long moment. The sky was every colour at once. Off in the west above the trees where they killed the bird, the falling sun spilt golden through a pane of clear sky. But the light drew every shade of grey out of the layers of cloud above. The silhouettes of the highest trees across the hillside were black. Between the shadows of their branches, the light filtered to a blood-red with laser beam precision. The red light cast long shadows down from the woods which almost reached the hillside and the horses.

Across the valley, against the tiny shadows of the old mills and the useless chimneys of the empty factories, the horizon had drained all the light. All that was left was a deep veil of purple which burnt to a crisp black and threatened to merge into the shadow of the city. Street lights began to signal their surrender.

Above them, at the point where the horses still roamed and the boys stood anchored to the ground, the light and the darkness waged war. It was clear which would win.

The foal shivered once more. The two boys watched.

'Reckon you can shoot 'em without 'em being sick?' Liam said.

'What?' Ryan said.

'If they were suffering 'n' that?'

'What d'you mean?' Ryan said. 'You shoot 'em when you can't save 'em. When it's kindest thing to do.'

'What if it's still kindest thing to do?' Liam said. 'You know, to stop it suffering 'n' that.'

The legs of the foal looked like branches ready to snap. They angled inwards like a tripod and the fragile body of the horse shivered to keep its balance upon them.

'What you on about?' Ryan said. His words were sincere.

Liam looked away from the foal and down to the ground.

'Dunno.' he said. 'They should put horses inside at night. You know, when it gets cold. Put 'em int stables.'

'Farmer dun't have stables,' Ryan said. 'He keeps 'em up here to toughen 'em up.'

'How d'you know?'

'Our Jamie told us,' Ryan said. 'Loads of them old ones used to die in winter. Even before all them ones what got shot.'

'Farmer's a cunt,' Liam muttered.

'Aye,' Ryan said.

'Better go, Ry,' Liam said.

'One minute,' Ryan said.

He looked at the horses. He looked at each horse in turn, resting his eyes upon them. He looked at the little foal and the little foal looked back at him. If he looked at the horses long enough, perhaps everything else would be okay. Perhaps everything else would grow warmer and safer and the things which had already happened might not already have happened.

'Why'd they kill horses but not people?' Liam said.

'What?' Ryan said.

'Like when people get sick 'n' that, no one shoots 'em.'

'Course they fucking don't,' Ryan said. 'What you gunna say if your gran's in hospital and doctor comes in and says it's time for the bolt gun?'

'Why'd they do it to horses then?' Liam said. 'Why not try and make them better 'n' all?'

Ryan looked from the horses down to the frosty ground. It was darker now and darkening still. The street lights on the edge of the estate down the hillside were a long way off. Nothing reached the darkness of the field. The cloud was thick. The night would not show moon or star.

'Dunno,' Ryan said. His voice was quiet and sad.

'Why'd they have to get sick for anyway?' Liam said.

'You know why they got sick,' Ryan said. 'Soil's fucked up here cos of quarry.'

'No, I mean, like, why?' Liam said. 'Why's it have to happen?'

'What you on about?'

'It's just shit, int it?' Liam said. He looked through the haze of darkness to the eye of the old, grey horse. 'You know what I mean though? Stuff like that's just proper shit.'

Ryan nodded.

'Like wi' your Jamie,' Liam said.

Ryan nodded.

'I don't get stuff like that,' Liam said. 'You know, stuff what's proper shit but just keeps happening?'

Ryan nodded.

He did not look at Liam. His face was sad. Liam's face was sad. The eyes of all the horses were sad and the sky was sad and dark and endless and brilliant and wild. They could not see the moon and stars but the moon and stars still were.

Ryan forced a smile. He looked at Liam.

'Here, right,' he said. 'If you were in charge, then, like if you were boss of it all, what would you do to sort it out?'

'What d'you mean?' Liam said.

'Like if you could sort it all out, right, what would you do?'

'If I were, whatsit? Prime Minister?'

Ryan shook his head.

'No, like if you were God or summat,' he said. 'Like if you had superpowers so you could sort it all out. What would you do?'

Liam smiled. His smile was sincere. He entertained the thought and threw it around in his mind.

'I'd make it so horses were alright,' he said. 'Make it so they're warm enough 'n' that and they wun't get sick.'

'How?' Ryan said.

Liam thought for a moment. 'Dunno,' he said. 'I'm in charge of it aren't I? Can do what the fuck I like.'

Ryan nodded. 'What else, then?' he said.

'I'd make thorns and brambles fuck off,' Liam beamed. 'That little short-arse pit bull 'n' all.'

'What, you'd kill dog if you were God?'

'Wun't kill it,' Liam said. 'Just make it so it weren't there. Same with dickheads 'n' that. You know like Macca and Danny and them lot?'

'I wun't,' Ryan said. 'I'd proper beat shit out of 'em. Little bastards.'

Liam nodded.

'What else would you do then?' Liam said.

Ryan was about to say something but he stopped himself.

'Dunno,' he said.

Liam paused.

'I'd get myself like a shitload of kebabs and loads of money 'n' all,' he said. 'Live in a proper big house and get myself a Lamborghini.' He beamed.

'You daft bastard,' Ryan laughed. 'You reckon God's just stuffing his face full of kebabs and driving around in his Lamborghini?'

A chilly wind came down across the field once more. Liam shivered and then Ryan shivered and the foal shivered and sheltered in against the fortress of its mother.

'Better go down, Ry,' Liam said.

'Aye, alright,' Ryan said.

They lingered for a moment more and looked at the horses through the veil of darkness and said nothing. Then they turned to walk back down the hillside.

They followed the retreating light but the retreating light had passed beyond the far horizon. In the sky above the woodland, the red light wrestled with the orange and the purple. It looked like the woods were ablaze. The air between the two boys was cold and misted with the whispered warning that the night would surely follow. Birds squawked to the falling sun and their echo emphasised the distance between the boys and the highest branches.

They left the field the way they had come. The grasses seemed thicker underfoot but the way across the field seemed shorter than before. The downward slope made their steps fall easy over the earth.

They reached the wooden fence. The four wooden beams still bore the mud left by the boys when they first had scaled it. Ryan stepped forward again and placed his muddy boot on the beam second from the bottom. He made to hoist himself over. Then something stopped him.

'Oh shit, Ry', Liam whispered suddenly. There was something terrible in his voice. 'Oh, fuck's sake,' he said. His voice sounded like tears and panic and dread. It sounded worse than it had sounded at any time before. Worse than when he saw the badger. Worse than when he saw the pit bull. Worse than when he had been frightened of the earth beneath the field.

Ryan turned to him. Liam's eyes were wide with the horror of whatever it was that he saw. He looked past Ryan, up along the fence-line to the dark shadows beneath the black trees.

Ryan turned to see what he was seeing.

Then he saw it.

CHAPTER NINE

The shadows from the mass of trees and the barer tree which stood apart bled into the encroaching night. The form of the thing the two boys saw merged with the land around it. But they saw it, sharp as the eye of a living bird.

A black horse lay dying in the darkness by the trees. It had fallen on to its side, its great back bared from the shadows to the boys. Its legs splayed out before and behind it. It lay dying, not dead. The two boys knew this.

Dying was unmistakable. You knew it before you knew how you knew. You saw it and you smelt it and the taste of it whispered up your nostrils and settled against your tongue and down your throat. Once you looked at dying you could not claim you looked at anything else.

The two boys looked at the horse in the distance beyond them. It was prostrate and splayed out and still. It lived but soon would die. They knew it. They knew this with some deep and ancient part of them. They knew it with the part of them they shared with their ancestors and their ancestors' ancestors back before the word had first been spoken. They knew death as the one thing surer than all else.

'Oh shit, Ry,' Liam said.

'S'alright,' Ryan spoke softly. He spoke like a father but not like his father.

'Oh shit,' Liam said again. He came back to himself a little and unfroze and looked from the horse to his friend and then back to the horse. 'Oh shit, Ry. What if its head's fucked like them ones what got shot?'

Ryan acknowledged the thought. He saw the old horses in his mind's eye, roaming like ghosts through the same field. The ones which had been culled. The memory of their heavy bodies walked among the living bodies of the horses through the darkness of the field. He remembered the men who had been sent by the council. He remembered them walking up the hillside. He remembered their bolt guns and the tents which had hidden the horses' deaths. He remembered the body of the old foal thrown limp into the back of the van while he and Jamie had stood and watched through the trees from the hillside. He remembered the way Jamie had watched and understood and not spoken.

'It's alright,' he said again. The softness in his voice spoke like a father to himself.

'Oh shit, Ry,' Liam said. He was panicked now. He looked back and forth from horse to Ryan to horse again. His eyes were wide and the air was dark and cold. 'I said we shun't come up here. I said them horses shun't be back here. Din't I say? My uncle said it's not safe. It's not right for 'em to be back here, Ry.'

'Just shut up,' Ryan said. The words carried a strange comfort. 'We don't know what's up with it, do we? Let's go have a look, it might've just fallen.'

'We shun't go up there, Ry. Oh shit. We need to just go. What if we're just spreading it around? My uncle said that's what can happen. You carry it round on your boots 'n' that.' His words came fast and sincere.

'What you on about?' Ryan said. 'We can't fucking leave it. What if its hurt 'n' we need to tell farmer?'

'Fuck's sake,' Liam whispered. He bit his lip and looked wide-eyed at the dying horse. Goosebumps rose along his arms and down the back of his neck with the strange curse whispered by the breeze.

'It's alright,' Ryan said. 'Come on.'

He jumped down from the beam of fence and his soles met the mud of the forbidden field once more.

They looked at the horse for a long moment. They stood and watched the heavy creature twitch against the vast earth in the distance up beyond. They stood and watched as if possessed.

'Come on,' Ryan said again. He said it to himself as much as to Liam.

The boys' steps compelled them up the long slope towards the beast. In spite of themselves and gravity and the slope and death and the shadows they kept walking. Up over the dark grass. Up through the purple mistings of the swelling night. Up towards the blackness of the barren trees. Up towards the horse.

It lay before and above them up the hillside like a black hole. It weighed above them like some great nothing which drew all life in towards it. It was the absence around which everything revolved and struggled in vain to avoid. It was the absence which proved by its absence that existence existed.

The two boys slowed as they drew nearer to the horse. Their breath quickened once more. They stopped and they stared at the giant beast. It thrashed one of its hind legs as Ryan made to kneel beside it. He stepped back. The animal kicked again, willing its huge useless body to sprint away.

'Alright boy,' Ryan whispered. He paused a few yards away from the great back of the horse. Its hind legs flinched but its two front legs could not move. They stretched out ahead of the wounded animal, grotesque in their uselessness. The black glossy eye glancing up at them was wild with terror. It reflected nothing.

'It's alright,' Ryan said. He could not get close enough to touch the horse. He did not dare. He spoke the words into the purple wind and did not know if he aimed them at himself or at Liam or at the horse or at the rest of the world. His voice was soft and thin and ready to break.

'Oh, fuck's sake, Ry,' Liam said. He slammed his eyes tight shut as if he was about to cry but he did not cry. He opened his eyes once more. They were red and tearless and wide. 'I don't like this, Ry. I don't like this.' His words came fast and sincere. He spoke like the child he was.

Ryan did not respond. He looked at the horse for an answer which was not there. In the light of day, the legs of the horses always looked spindly and precise. But close as the two boys were to the fallen black horse, its legs looked strong enough to kill. It twitched and thrashed again and its hind-legs kicked back into nothing. It wanted to leave but it could not leave. Its two front legs stretched off before it like snapped fingers. Useless. There was no movement left in them. It was not clear if its legs were broken or if the sickness meant its brain no longer willed them on.

Its hind legs still worked. The impulse to escape thundered out of the mad mind of the horse into those back legs once more. They kicked and kicked and kicked but the great horse did not move. It whined and grunted in panic.

'What we gunna do, Ry?' Liam said. His eyes were wide. 'Oh, fuck's sake. Is it gunna die?'

'Just shut up,' Ryan said. 'I'm trying to think, aren't I?' His eyes were wider, too, and he looked down at the vast horse like a child. He glanced across the field to where the other horses continued to wander with their mouths to the earth. The horizon had drained all the light and the man they feared who owned the field was nowhere to be seen. Ryan looked again at the eye of the horse. It was desolate and black. Its coat shimmered and staggered across its belly like a vast, dark lake. The animal grunted its pain while the two boys stared down. They were small beside the body of the beast.

He took a small step up towards the head of the horse and away from the dying anger of its hind legs. He lowered himself to a crouch and reached his small hand out to rest against the warm space between the horse's ears. The ears twitched in agitation and its hind legs kicked out at nothing once more. Ryan kept his hand resting in place, soft against the creature's head.

'It's alright, boy,' he said again but he did not believe his own words. Liam did not believe them, either. The horse did not believe in anything beside the instinct of its pain and the madness which fevered in its mind. Its eye was black and deranged and afraid. The moon and stars may still have believed but the moon and stars were a long way from the field.

Ryan blinked and then shut his eyes as though he was about to cry but he did not cry. Up by the head of the horse, there was no way for its hind legs to hurt him. He opened his eyes again. He looked at the mad eye of the horse. He felt again what he had felt when he had buried the bird. The sadness of everything. In the eye of the horse. In the black tree. In the face of his friend. You could pretend it was not there but it was always there and it always had been and it always still would be. The sadness of everything.

He leant forward and wrapped his skinny arms around the head of the horse. He held the giant creature with his small hands.

'It's alright,' he said again. 'It's alright, boy.'

Then he cried. He knelt against the hard ground and hugged the head of the horse and he cried.

Liam looked down with wide eyes at the dying creature and the tears in the eyes of his friend. Ryan cradled the horse's head like he had cradled the bird. His tears were silent.

'It's okay,' he said and his arms and his hands warmed with the warmth in the head of the horse. He hugged the horse's head soft and close. The madness in the great beast's eye settled just a little. It kicked another kick but there was less desperation in the kick this time.

'Shh, boy,' Ryan said. 'It's okay.'

He held the horse until the worst of the panic breathed out of it. It was frightened still. The animal was nothing but instinct. Everything was as it was. The panic. The desperation. The pain. There was no pretending it was anything else. But there was also the comfort of the boy's arms around it. Thick cloud covered the night sky but there was also the starlight far above.

'It's okay,' Ryan whispered once more. He let the horse go and he stood up. He wiped the tears away with the backs of his muddy hands and he did not cry again.

Both boys looked down at it and did not speak.

'Reckon we should go tell farmer?' Liam said. His words wavered and the air was cold.

Ryan shook his head.

'Farmer's a dickhead,' he said. 'He'll beat shit out of you for coming up here. Then he'll have to go shoot rest of horses 'n' all.'

'Just gunna leave it then?' Liam said.

Ryan shrugged and said nothing.

It was one thing to watch a bird die. It was one thing to see the body of one so small. It was one thing to watch a man die. But this horse was bigger than a man. It was bigger than any man had ever been. It was sadder and stronger and darker and more brilliant and more desperate and more anguished and alive. It could not die. They could not stand and watch it die.

Ryan reached for the neck of the gun. He did this before he had time to think it through. He swung the thing on its belt from his shoulder and into his hands. He pointed it at the head of the horse.

'What you doing?' Liam said.

Ryan said nothing. He exhaled sharply and tried to steady himself. He lowered his eye to the aim.

'You won't kill it wi' that.' Liam said.

Ryan placed his bony finger on the trigger and centred the aim straight at the head of the horse. The warmth of the beast still remained on the palms of his hand but the wind was sharp and cold.

'Don't, Ry,' Liam said. 'You won't kill it wi' that.'

'Just shut up!' Ryan said.

He squinted through the aim at the head of the giant horse.

'Let's just go, Ry,' Liam said.

Ryan saw again in his mind's eye the limp body of the foal. He had watched as it was thrown like meat into the back of the van. Jamie had watched it too. They had heard the shot but had not seen it. He remembered the wound. The black and bloodied hole at the top of the animal's head. Right between its ears. The same point at which he had rested his hand on the black horse before him.

He found that point in his aim. He held the aim a long while and exhaled and inhaled deep breaths of the bitter air.

'Just leave it, Ry,' Liam spoke softly. Through the misting darkness the other horses were heavy and living and sad. They did not look at the boys.

'Can't just leave it,' Ryan said.

'You won't kill it with that,' Liam said. He looked from Ryan to the huge horse.

Ryan pointed the gun for a long while at the head of the beast. It continued to whine and its black eye continued to glisten with the dark glow of nothing. The neck of the gun trembled in his hand.

'You won't kill it,' Liam said again. He spoke like there were tears in his eyes but there were none.

The horse kicked its hind legs once more. Instinct compelled it. Ryan placed his finger against the trigger. He tried to steady himself but he was growing agitated with the desperate creature.

'Just leave it, Ry,' Liam said. His words were softer now. He looked at his friend.

Ryan stared at the frightened animal. The two boys were small beneath the dark and endless sky. The horse's hooves continued to kick, pounding muddy dents into the cold ground. Ryan looked across towards the other horses. They had almost been taken by the darkness. He lowered his gun and looked at the earth.

CHAPTER TEN

They walked away without a word. They walked back the way they had come before turning and heading down towards the edge of the estate. Everything had darkened as they went through the silent web of roads past the rows of watching windows under the violent sky. Between the houses, the hill leading up to the quarry glimpsed back into view. The woods stared down at them. The specks of the horses roaming the forbidden field hung over the estate, ever-present on the hillside while the streets were still.

All night long the horse would lie there in the shadow of the trees. Its eye would stare into the blackness. It would kick and twitch and try to run. Maybe it would die. Maybe it would last until morning when the owner would find and shoot it.

The sickness would spread. It came out of the ground. It lived in the soil then it lived in the grasses. It jumped into the bodies of the horses and it wormed its way into their brains.

The cold evening air demanded more breath as the boys stepped over the grey pavement. Each second moved them further from the horses and back down into everything. But something had been lost and everything had changed. The houses. The empty rooms. The words they would go back to. Everything buckled with the huge weight of the horse.

Overhead, the pigeons flew without formation. The two boys stared at the ground as they walked.